Poolnabrone,

County Clare

"Pool of sorrows."

Mona, the body in the bog
By
Loretto Horrigan Leary

Cover art and interior artwork by
Jeff Buckholz

Ireland
ULSTER
CONNAUGHT
MEATH
Eber's
Half
LEINSTER
MUNSTER

Suspend, willingly, your disbelief.

Published May 16, 2013

Mona,

the Body in the Bog

by

Loretto Horrigan Leary

Although the places exist, the bog body does not. This story is a work of fiction. Any resemblance to any persons living or dead is coincidental.

On March 17, 2009, to mark International Women's Day, *L'Osservatore Romano*, the Vatican's official newspaper said that the washing machine liberated women.

For Kevin.

Front cover and interior art by Jeff Buckholz

May 2013

The Meeting

He had never seen the symbol of the triune goddess on anyone but his wife. Lying on the beach here before him was a defeated Fir Bolg with the triune goddess symbol dangling from his neck; three intertwined silver leaves glittered in the golden, sinking sunlight.

A hand reached up to touch the Irish Celt's tunic. The sun blinded the fallen warrior's eyes; the figure standing before the Fir Bolg warrior was a black silhouette, a stark contrast to the brightness surrounding him.

The waves rolled behind the wounded Fir Bolg warrior, crashing against his back, knocking him off balance. Again his hand reached for the tunic, but slipped. Instead, he grabbed the checkered braccae that stuck to the Irish Celt's legs as each crashing wave splashed against the muscular calves.

The spear, a thin wooden shaft, its iron point projected at an angle for a downward stab, was a terrifying threat to the Fir Bolg, lying half raised on his left arm, helpless and defeated. The spear remained aloft, ready to strike at any moment, instilling fear into the Fir Bolg, yet he refused to show it. The warriors from his tribe, the Belgae, were trained to die nobly. But alone on the beach with his Irish enemy before him, his eyes betrayed him. Though he struggled to show no fear, his eyes were alight with it. The silhouette of his enemy loomed above him, like a lightning bolt ready to strike at any moment.

The warrior on the sand was a Fir Bolg, a Celt from northern mainland Europe, young and fierce. Although he had dealt vicious blows with his sword toward the Irish Celt now standing before him, the Fir Bolg warrior did not give up easily.

His outstretched hand now grasped the braccae of his Irish enemy, but not in a threatening move; the Irish Celt could see that the Fir Bolg was weakened. The attempt to invade Ireland's shores from the south of the island had failed for the Fir Bolg. The Irish had defended their shores successfully, this time.

The Irish Celt moved forward, extending his hand to the warrior. Although he was at least ten years older than his Fir Bolg counterpart, the two men had fought a fair battle, and now one would leave a victor and the other would die. This was the world of warriors, and both men knew it well.

The outstretched hand grabbed the wrist of the Fir Bolg. Blood streamed down his forearm; when it hit the elbow, it dripped furiously to the sand, staining it a deep brownish red. Believing that his enemy would perish on the beach, the Irish man prepared to give the final, fatal stab. He lifted his foot from the sand, and then resting it on the defeated warrior's left shoulder; he shoved down with his foot. The Fir Bolg felt his body press into the wet sand, which was now hard like stone. The Irish Celt threw his spear aside and his right hand reached for his scabbard, withdrawing a small sword with a wide blade.

The Irish warrior dropped to his knees and grabbed the long, blond, wet hair of the Fir Bolg. Grasping the sword even tighter, the Irish Celt pulled the hair back with his left hand and positioned the sharp blade of his sword below the area of the Fir Bolg's neck, where the beard hairs were short and the skin was smooth.

His hand pushed on the blade, applying pressure to the skin; a trickle of blood appeared, dribbling over the silver triune goddess symbol sparkling in the sun, both silver and blood. It was the same triune goddess symbol as the one that the Irish Celt, Diarmuid, wore on his wrist.

Releasing the pressure of the sword, he looked at his wrist. The leather strap was blood stained, but the symbol of the triune goddess shone in the sunlight. He had never seen anyone else wear this symbol, only his own wife, Etain. It was she who had given it to him.

The Irish Celt removed the sword, shifted his grip from the Fir Bolg's hair to the cloth at the front of his chest and pulled him to standing. When they were face to face, the Irish Celt began speaking in a tongue similar to the Fir Bolg warrior's own language.

"My wife reveres all life. Today I have killed my last man. If I spare you, it is because of this." He shook the wristlet on his left arm. "Birth, life and death, do you understand?"

The Fir Bolg nodded. He recognized the wristlet's three intertwined leaf symbols. The Irish Celt took a step backwards; he stretched out his hand and placed it on the Fir Bolg's left shoulder.

"Live," he said. "Today you will live!" Then he stepped away, turning toward the mainland, and disappearing into the forest.

The Fir Bolg watched his enemy walk away, and then he collapsed back into the damp, stony sand, semi-conscious on the shores of Cork, in the south of Ireland.

In sixteen years, the two men would meet again, but only one would be spared.

Mona, the body in the bog

Chapter 1

Liam sat for what seemed like hours. As he stomped the cigarette butt into the sod a thought crossed his mind. What if he had just cut through hundreds of bodies at a burial site?

He lifted his gaze from the foot below and scanned the flat lands of the bog. Beneath the heather and gorse bushes that grew and blossomed all around this bog, there could be an ancient burial site that he had discovered today.

The wind whipped the heather forward, making the purple flowers shake wildly. It wouldn't be the first time that a body had been discovered in a bog. Liam remembered the bog body found in the 1980s, in Lindow, England. He was just finishing secondary school, and his science teacher was very excited about the bog body discovery in England.

"It's amazing what you remember, too," Liam thought to himself as he nodded and looked at the foot. At the age of thirty eight, he still remembered how his science teacher of almost

twenty years previous had talked about the “Lindow Man” as if he were an international hero like Neil Armstrong.
The discovery of the bog body in Lindow Moss bog in England by professional peat cutters in 1984 was big news. Liam was waiting for the results of his Leaving Cert. On August 1 1984, the brutal death of an Iron Age bog body was briefly more important than the exam results.

Liam’s thoughts were interrupted by a siren in the distance becoming louder and louder. It was definitely heading his way. “Thank God.” A sigh of relief departed his lungs vigorously, and he turned his gaze away from the foot and searched the headland of the bog for the garda car.

When the garda car arrived fifteen minutes later, the sirens were wailing and the lights were flashing. When the call had come in to the Borrisokane barracks announcing a suspected homicide at Boteen’s bog in North Tipperary, the two gardaí on duty jumped into motion. They pulled their feet from the tops of their desks and threw on their navy blue jackets, pulled their caps tightly onto their heads, and promptly began to search through the mess of paper work for the keys to the garda car.

“You respond that we’re on our way, I’ll get the car started,” said Sergeant Hannon, unable to believe his luck; he had found the keys in less than fifteen seconds! What a record!

Like the Keystone cops in hyperactive mode, the two Borrisokane gardaí shot from the barracks to the garda car and tore madly through the town with blaring sirens, beeping at anyone foolish enough to get in their way. The pedestrians stared in disbelief at the speeding garda car as it raced through the town. Some shook their heads disapprovingly, while others commented aloud.

"Ever heard of a speeding limit, lads?"

Liam had smoked five cigarettes by the time they arrived. His eyes were bloodshot and rimmed with tears, not from crying, mind you, but more from the strain of having his stomach convulse occasionally and staring at the foot. He had not dared look away from it for too long.

When he saw the garda car come to a stop on the solid strip of headland, Liam's gaze returned to the foot. He hadn't taken his eyes from the scene until he had heard the siren of the garda car. He had stared at the foot the whole time, for two reasons; one, he was absolutely terrified to look away, and two, the skin. There was something odd about the skin. Either this foot belonged to someone who wasn't Irish, or it had been in the bog for quite a long time. This was definitely not a fairly new dead foot protruding from the sod; the skin was very different indeed. He might be right about the burial site after all. The leathery look of the skin was creepy in and of itself, but the fact that the foot was sticking straight up out of the ground like that made him imagine a cross section of the bog where the body was. The head straight down and the feet sticking straight up. Was this body inserted into the bog upside down?

The two gardaí took long swift strides and made their way deliberately toward the machine. Liam and his discovery were obscured from their view. As the gardaí rounded the side of the turf-cutting machine, they both removed their caps simultaneously and tucked them under their left armpits.

"Well, lo and behold!" came the smoky, resonant voice of Sergeant Hannon, as the foot came into his view.

There it was. It was almost as if the foot was signaling at them from the ground, as if it wanted to be found, sticking straight up.

The youngest garda pulled a small black notebook from his top left coat pocket and retrieved a pencil from the spiral. Unable to take his gaze off the foot, he began to question Liam and take notes at the same time.
Hannon walked closer to the foot and knelt down beside it. He felt the dampness of the sod creep through his trousers and his knees felt cold. He breathed in deeply through his nose and blew out a sigh through clenched teeth. His fleshy top lip

seemed to disappear into his mouth as his bottom lip enveloped it. This was Hannon's characteristic look of "I just don't believe my own eyes."

Hannon pulled a pen from his top left pocket and poked the foot. The flesh was supple and fresh. Then he bent his head a little closer and sniffed; there was no smell of decay. This was a perfect foot. The toenails were all intact, and even a couple of hairs on the big toe were visible. Despite the fact that the skin was supple, there was no smell or sign of deterioration; it was a strange color, though, almost like leather.

"This foot is not a recent deposit in this bog bank," Hannon mused to himself. He was secretly delighted that he was able to put *deposit* and *bog bank* into the same sentence, so delighted, in fact, that he pushed himself to standing and, turning towards his onlookers said, "This body isn't a recent deposit in this bog bank, I'd say."

Some thought Sergeant Hannon was an extremely witty person, while others called him "a dry bollocks." His humor therefore was not appreciated by everyone. He turned his back to the two men and bent toward the foot again. This was definitely not his gig. He knew this was a job for the Limerick Homicide Unit. Hannon turned his head slightly so that he could hear the question and answer session in progress behind him.

"No, I didn't move the machine an inch since I called 999" Liam stated without emotion.

"That was about twenty minutes ago, right?" said the younger garda, still writing copiously in his little black notebook.

"Tis all right, Mick," yelled Hannon, as he strode in their direction. "We don't have the killer on our hands here."

"What makes you say that, Sarge?" Mick replied.

"Well," said Hannon, putting his pen into his breast pocket and shoving his hands deep into his trouser pockets for greater effect. "First and foremost, don't call me sarge, and secondly, my guess is lads that this foot here—," turning toward the direction of the foot and removing his hands from his pocket to point at it, just in case they'd forgotten which foot he was referring to. "This foot here has been stuck in the mud for a long, long, long time."

With each "long" his voice grew deeper and deeper, and the word itself became longer and longer. The dramatic effect was tremendous, in Hannon's opinion.

Liam was no-where near to being impressed by the sergeant's powers of deduction. "You don't have to be Sherlock Holmes to

figure that one out," said Liam, as he watched the sergeant jingle the coins, and God knows what else, in his trouser pockets.
Hannon was high on his own power over the scene. Liam's "Sherlock Holmes" comment went unheard. Liam decided to play along. "Let's hear what Ireland's own Sherlock Holmes thinks," Liam thought to himself.

"Well, Sherlock, what do you think happened here?"

Still high on his self-importance, Hannon spouted on. "I think we have a bog body here," he said.

Liam, the machinist, and Mick the young garda were seemingly *astounded* at the sergeant's powers of deduction. Mick was genuinely flabbergasted at how smart the sergeant was. Liam, on the other hand, had heard rumors of the "dry bollocks of a sergeant from Borrisokane," so he was enjoying the display of knowledge from Hannon.

Liam and Mick both looked from the foot to the sergeant and then back to the foot again. Liam waited for the famous Sherlock Holmes line, "Elementary, my dear Watson," and half expected the sergeant to produce an ornate smoking pipe and hunting cap. But as the sergeant was momentarily speechless, a

short silence passed, and then Liam remembered his own thoughts earlier: The burial site, an ancient burial site.
"I wonder if this was a burial site or something like that?" he said, looking from one garda to the other. Both shrugged their shoulders and then returned their gaze to the foot. Then two things struck Liam simultaneously.

"How do you know he's been here for a long time, Sergeant?" he asked. Surely the sergeant could not have deduced all of that just by looking and taking a quick sniff? This would be interesting, worthy of a moment or two of actually focusing seriously to see how the sergeant came up with his theories.

"Two things, lads, just two things. The skin has been preserved by the bog, that's why it's a funny color, you know? Have you ever seen a cow hide at a tannery when it is being made into leather? Looks just like this." He turned again toward the foot and started taking in the view of the bog.

"So it's fairly old, then?" asked Mick, staring at the sergeant.
"I'd say that Liam here might have found a bog body, like the one they found in Drumkeeragh Bog in County Down a few years back. And I'd say it is a male."

"Right," both Mick and Liam chimed in simultaneously, but Mick truly had no clue as to what the sergeant had just made reference to. Better to agree than to appear stupid. Liam, on the other hand, was genuinely surprised this time at Hannon's ability to recall a bog body find in Ireland. "Then again," he thought, "the sergeant could just be making this up to impress his current audience." Mick was easy to impress, but Liam was a tougher client.

"And the reason you know it's a male?" Liam asked, eager to hear Sergeant Hannon's reasoning.

"The feet are rough, too rough to be a woman's, and too wide, too. They have to belong to a man. I'd bet money on it. I am certain that this is out of our league. This is a job for the Limerick homicide unit and we'll let them take it from here."

Now totally and utterly convinced of his "on-the-money" theories about the body attached to the foot, Hannon continued with theatrical flair.

"The museum people will want to send archaeologists and specialists as soon as possible to retrieve the foot, and whatever is attached to it."

"This was an impressive speech indeed," thought Hannon as he turned his attention to Mick, who was still writing furiously in his little black book.

"Call the Limerick barracks and have a Homicide detective report to the scene here. Have them contact the National Museum and get those people involved, too." Hannon enjoyed giving orders. That was the best part of his job.

The calls were made to Limerick and Dublin; first to the regular Dublin gardaí and then, in turn, to the "museum people." Mick O'Brien, Hannon's sidekick, called the Limerick homicide unit. Explaining the find in terse detail, but being careful not to leave anything out; O'Brien assured them that all persons would remain on the scene until the arrival of the detective from Limerick.

The Limerick homicide detective arrived within fifty minutes of the phone call to the Limerick garda barracks. The journey to Booteen's bog was done with full sirens blaring and at a speed of about eighty miles an hour.

The detective almost crashed his car into the stone wall of the narrow bridge, which was described to him as a final landmark. He was told to look for the laneway entrance to the bog, which would be on his right shortly after coming over the bridge. It didn't help that the detective had crossed the bridge at eighty miles an hour!
A tractor trailer packed high with bags of turf was directly in front of the detective when he suddenly realized he was on the

wrong side of the road. Abruptly, he pulled the steering wheel of the squad car to the right, at about the same time that the farmer driving the tractor jerked his steering wheel to the left, sending a seismic shift down the trailer, and dislodging turf from the top of the heap. "Ding, bang, thump!" The squad car was rained on by a hail of dislodged turf.

"Jazus Christ!" The detective roared at the top of his lungs, desperately trying to negotiate the road ahead between lumps of brown turf, giant tractor wheels, and the farmer screaming, "Ya fucking ejit!"

The squad car cleared the agricultural obstacle course, the homicide detective regained control of the car, and then he saw the laneway entrance to Booteen's bog on the right.

Now traveling at a relative "snail's pace" of fifty-five miles per hour, sirens still filling the air with their shrill call, the car made its way slowly down the lane way. This time, the detective kept close to the right side of the lane. Briars and brambles scraped along the right side of the squad car, but after almost colliding head on with a turf-filled tractor trailer, Detective Riordan wasn't taking any chances. Better to get a few scrapes and scratches on the car than to end up under the front wheel of a tractor.

Once the view in his window changed from an archway of hanging tree branches and grabbing bramble bushes to the broader horizon of a flat, expansive bog-land, Riordan felt safe. He brought the car to a stop next to the Police car.

Riordan's preloaded crime scene bag was pulled laboriously from the trunk. It weighed a ton with all the cameras and equipment inside. By the time Riordan was walking toward the three men gathered by the turf cutter, a helicopter was hovering overhead.

Riordan looked heavy with his paraphernalia, and he seemed to sink deeper into the bog with each step he took. He was a big man, about six foot two. He shook hands with the gardaí and then spoke to Liam. Notes were jotted down feverishly, and then a camera, tape recorder, and measuring tape were whisked from the bag. The foot was photographed from every angle. He knew almost immediately, by the leathery look of the skin, that it was not a recent death.

Once landmarks such as the Portumna swivel bridge had been given and acknowledged as recognizable from the air, the Dublin squad was on the move. By the time the Limerick homicide detective had finished observing the scene and the foot, the helicopter had landed a little distance away from the squad cars, on solid ground, and the people inside were spilling out onto the headland of the bog.

***

When the helicopter picked Maire Moylan up, the two assisting archeologists were already seated in the helicopter, one in front, with the pilot, and the other behind. The effects of the prescription pills she had taken only three hours earlier were kicking in, and the prospect of a flight in a claustrophobic helicopter for the next thirty minutes or so was not appealing.

Up until a month ago, Maire had believed that she could do and have it all. Hard work had got her to where she was today. If she could get a good job at the museum through hard work and dedication, then she could get pregnant with hard work and dedication. “There are no obstacles, only the ones we create,” she had often told herself during times of stress.

The fertility clinic doctor had told her three weeks ago that she had a condition called polycystic ovarian syndrome and that this was the reason for her inability to get pregnant or stay pregnant. He said it so matter-of-factly, that Maire thought it must be common enough, and not too serious. After the doctor wrote out her prescription and warned her of the side effects of the pills, she thought nothing more of it.

"Surely the pills were as mild as the condition itself," she had hoped. Nothing could be further from the truth.
The nausea, mood swings, and hot flashes had taken over her life to almost the same level of intensity as getting pregnant had. There was no more "love making" in her marriage. There was "Come on will ya! I've got to get to work. Hurry up!"

Only five minutes into the flight the nausea had settled in, and to add to her troubles, her mood swings were getting under way. She almost screamed at the pilot midflight, but she imagined him doing flips and turns to spite her if she mentioned her nausea. She resisted the urge to tell him to "Fly the bloody machine straight, ya loser!" instead rummaging through her duffel bag, hoping to distract her attention from the disappearing and reappearing horizon.

The occasional air pocket drop vaulted her stomach into her throat; keeping her head bent, she felt like she had tied a fifty-pound weight to her skull. When the pilot announced, rather nasally, "I see it now," she almost broke into a round of applause, but decided that gripping onto the side of her seat for dear life was a better idea.

The assisting archaeologists perceived her swift bolt from the helicopter as pure dedication to the job. In reality, she was hard pressed not to do a papal ground-kissing ritual as she exited the helicopter and felt solid ground beneath her feet!

***

It had now been about sixty-seven minutes since Liam had made his discovery. As the helicopter whipped the heather and gorse bushes into violently animated things and then slowly dropped to the flattest and clearest part of the bog, the crowd already gathered at the scene looked on in astonishment. Doors opened, and three figures emerged, stooping low to avoid the whirling blades.

Clutching black duffel bags and holding onto hats and coats, the three people made their way to Liam, the two Borrisokane gardaí the detective from Limerick and of course, the subject of the gathering, the foot.

Everyone introduced themselves quickly and shook hands without even looking at faces. The person from the National Museum was drawing a lot of attention from the crowd. Her auburn hair fell loosely onto her shoulders as her hat fell to the ground. After she had gathered all the information about how the body was discovered and what had happened since then, she asked one of the men with her to start taking notes from each person. Hannon was stunned. He couldn’t resist. He simply had to ask her what she did.

"Forensic archaeology," she responded curtly. "Your name again, please?"

"Hannon" he replied briskly, not at all amused that she had forgotten his name.
"Well, Sergeant Hannon, I am Maire Moylan, the forensic archaeologist in charge of this investigation. Thank you for watching over the scene here. I appreciate that the body has not been touched."

Then Maire looked from face to face. "We might need some help getting the body dug out before the weather turns bad, if you don't mind waiting around for a bit longer?"

They all nodded in agreement. They were as curious as she was about the body attached to the foot. Maire was relieved that the nausea had subsided and threw herself into full-on working mode. Hannon, on the other hand, stood powerless with shock.

She began unzipping and forcing the duffel bags wide open. The wind was picking up a bit, and the weather looked like it was going to change for the worse. Luminescent silvery clouds began to drift over the bog. She was too busy removing small shovels and a large black plastic body bag from her black duffel to even notice that her hat had fallen off. The five local men slowly shifted their gaze from the foot to this strange woman down on her hunkers rummaging through her duffel bag, her long, auburn, curly hair blowing madly in the wind.

The detective from Limerick asked her if she believed, like him, that this was not a modern-day body.
"It clearly is not," she said.

"I still need to hang on to take pictures of what we can't see under the surface right now, though," he said, knowing that she was more knowledgeable about the excavation that was about to get underway. She had her own camera and would continue taking pictures as the body was dug out.

"It is not a modern-day body," she said to him, "So we'll step in now and treat it as an archaeological find."

"Grand, then, but I will remain to take notes and pictures to complete the case on my end," the homicide detective said.

"No problem at all," Maire said, loading up hands and arms with various digging implements.

"I'll give you a hand there," he said, offering to take the load from her.

"Thanks a million. You can leave them down over there beside the foot." Her stomach churned a little. She took a deep breath and the nausea subsided. "Focus, focus, focus," she reminded herself, swallowing the bile that forced its way up her throat and into her mouth.

The other five men watched silently as the homicide detective from Limerick escorted the woman over to the foot. She secured a surgical mask's elastic around her ears and positioned the mask over her nose and mouth. Next, she pulled on green latex gloves. She pushed her hair back over her shoulders and secured it in a haphazard ponytail so it would not hang in her way. She carried the plastic bag and a shovel with her. Moylan didn't have to wear the surgical mask, but it had been a dry three weeks in the west of Ireland, so she knew that the bog's surface would be dusty. The fine particles of turf dust were easily inhaled and left a nasty, dry cough which could last for days, maybe even weeks.

The wind wasn't helping matters, as it made the dust become airborne before she had even sliced a sod. To the men from Portumna and Borrisokane, she looked like a woman preparing to come in contact with a deadly disease. Liam, Hannon, and Mick eyed each other suspiciously, wondering in silence if they too should request full body protection! Hannon, especially, was eager to jump into anything that resembled a space suit and would make him look more important.

Slowly and delicately she began to slice through the soft turf around the foot. Bog was an easy material to dig through, like slicing through sponge cake. It was soft, and there was little effort in taking turf away from the foot and revealing the leathery calf. Where did this body begin and where did it end? The real problem: Did this body get buried upside down, or did it somehow get mangled in all sorts of directions, and how do we unearth it all in one piece? Maire's mind raced with questions.

Secretly she hoped that the body had remained untouched and intact. This was a very rare opportunity for a forensic archaeologist, and she wanted to experience every nuance of it to the fullest. Bog bodies were not an everyday find, and she knew she was fortunate to be in charge of this one.

In the background, the sergeant, the young garda, and Liam continued to stare at the detective from Limerick, the Dublin specialists, and the young woman crouched over the foot, slowly revealing more of the leg with her tiny shovel.

"We'll have it unearthed in no time!" she called back over her shoulder, revealing still more of the thigh now.

"The land is very spongy and cuts easily. I will need help hoisting it into the bag, though."
The bog around her was dusty and dry and crumbly. The full leg was now visible.

"Great!" she yelled, "this is great!" Standing upright, she walked toward the three locals by the turf cutting machine. "I will need your help lifting it onto the body bag shortly, if that is okay?"

She retrieved another implement, a large, blunt, wide-bladed knife from her duffel bag and turned eagerly to reveal more of the strange treasure hidden in the bog.

"Yeah," Mick offered, a beat too slow.

"Sure," Liam added, ready to jump in and help.

"No problem, Missus," Hannon said, but he wasn't too keen on handling the body.

It was amazing to each of the local men to see a woman work fearlessly, knowingly, and obviously deeply interested in an area that up until now each one would have imagined being performed by a bearded, pipe-smoking and tweed-wearing old man.

"This is a strange new world we live in, lads, when a woman can do this kind of work without getting kinda queasy!" said Sergeant Hannon, unaware that she was close enough to hear his comment.
"If you are a little *queasy* with this type of thing, you don't have to help. I understand some people don't have the stomach for this stuff. We'll manage with the three of us here," she said motioning with the big blunt knife toward herself and the Dublin lads.

"No, we're grand. We're just amazed to see a woman do such a gruesome job! I suppose we were expecting a man to dig the body out, you know what we mean, like?" said Liam, suddenly aware of his thick Galway accent in juxtaposition to this woman's refined tone, neutral of any Irish county connection, and then realizing he had probably given her a very great insult.

"I don't mean it like that, but…," he quickly tried to rectify his statement and make it less harmful, but the truth was it was strange. A young woman digging out a body, and not having the slightest sign of it affecting her was odd to see. "She must be one tough woman," he thought.

"No harm meant!" he sheepishly called to her.

"None taken!" she called back, slicing out a block of sod about three feet wide, four feet long, and two feet deep around the body. He saw that she was smiling and was relieved she had not taken insult.

"What can we do to help?" he asked.

"I just need to determine the way the body is situated. As soon as I find out the angle, we can start digging. I'll need some of your help," Maire said, secretly hoping that she would know the answer to that question very soon. The queasiness was coming and going, and digging a body out of a bog was not helping to ease the problem.

It wasn't the first time she had received strange looks when people found out her profession, and she knew it would not be the last time either. Maire didn't mean to challenge society. Her own mother was a farmer's wife who cooked, cleaned, and worked on the farm, like many other Irish women.

Maire, a completely different type of woman than her mother, always had a passion for biology and physiology. Having witnessed many a lambing season and cows birthing, she was far from being the type of woman to swoon at the sight of blood. She had known since watching the annual "Calor Cosingas Housewife of the Year Competition" at the age of fourteen that she would never delight in baking the perfect strawberry rhubarb pie and flapping around a kitchen stove in a flowery apron, much to her mother's disappointment.

"We'll need to dig around the body and make sure that we leave some sod still around it if we can, to preserve it better until we get it back to Dublin," she instructed the two men assisting her. "The deeper I dig, the moister the sod is going to be, of course, so we will have to be very careful where we step."

By now the clouds had rolled over the landscape, and the colors of the bog and its foliage had changed. The atmosphere seemed to have altered, now seemingly in sympathy with the events unfolding in the bog. The mood shifted from innocent discovery to sinister find.

A drizzle of rain began sprinkling on the crowd. It was obvious that the weather was going to change to a heavier rain shortly. The colors of the heather, gorse, and bog took on an eerie glow, the low rain clouds adding a silvery unearthliness to the surroundings.

Maire mumbled something inaudible; the two men beside her arose and walked toward the duffel bags. Each brought out a larger shovel.

"Do ye want to help, lads?" they asked as they pulled out two more shovels.

"Right. We will, then." said Hannon, "Grab a shovel there, Mick, and start digging."

Sergeant Hannon preferred to observe the goings-on, seeing as no protective gear was being offered; he decided to play it safe and sent Mick in to do the dirty work.

"Give me one, too" said Liam, eager to unveil his discovery and play his part in this great pub story of the future. There'd be great mileage out of this one!
The weather was definitely taking a turn for the worse.

"Dig in a circumference of about four feet around me please," Maire said. "If this rain gets worse, we will just cut away a square of the bog and load it into a truck. Someone organize a truck to be on standby for us here locally. A truck that has a cover on it." Maire continued to clear away the sod as she spoke.

"Hopefully, if the rain doesn't get much worse than this, we might be able to uncover the body and bring it back to Dublin on the helicopter."

Hannon realized that he was in charge of getting a truck to remain on standby. He sprang into action, returning to the squad car and contacting the Borrisokane barracks. Within two minutes of conversation, the truck was arranged.

Now, fully over the shock of a woman doing a man's job, Liam, Mick, and the two specialists from Dublin, along with the Limerick homicide detective, Riordan, and under the guidance of the seemingly fearless young woman, slowly, gently, and cautiously revealed a full body still surrounded by clumps of peat from Booteen's bog.

The sad truth emerged with each shovelful of sod that was cast aside. A deeper and sadder truth was being uncovered along with the body.

The body had been buried upside down. The head was submerged first in the quick-sand-like soft peat. As each layer of sod was removed, another part of the body was revealed. The clothes, remnants of animal pelts, a woolen cloak, and what used to be to be a white linen tunic, were all in fair condition.

The thighs and calves now showed, covered in slashes, like whip marks, slicing deep into the flesh. A stiff rope-like material protruded through holes in the upper calves, near the knees. The soft drizzle was now a steady rain.

Three men positioned themselves to hold the corners of a large rectangle of black plastic over the scene in order to prevent the rain from damaging the clothing or the body itself.

The body was exposed to the waist, and Maire unrolled a black polyurethane body bag onto the ground. The body lay a-top of the bag; half the body, from waist to head, still remained submerged beneath the bogland.

This body had been brutalized, whipped, and buried upside down. Even without the help of forensic science, the brutality of the death was evident just by uncovering the body and simply looking at it.

As they dug deeper and deeper and slid the plastic bag under the body, the mood slipped into a somber sadness.
All parts of the body were intact. The skin was as supple as on the day it had been buried. The position of the body was evident now as the fully clothed corpse lay on the plastic. The clothes were very old and ornate. The top was a tunic of deep red, with bands of gold on what remained of the sleeves and on the hemline and the square neckline. Designs, like those in the Book of Kells were engrained in the gold bands: interlocking swirls with no beginning or end, and strange-looking half-human, half-animal beings in mighty poses, preserved for posterity in this beautifully intricate gold-band trim, most of it

hidden beneath layers of sod or decayed. There was no doubt that this tunic, remnant though it might be, was going to be a sight to behold once the sod had been cleaned away from it. After almost an hour and a half of digging, the discovery, though a treasure in many ways, was a tragedy.
The hands were tied behind the back. The upper arms had the same holes with stiff braided rope remnants visible in the wounds as those in the calves of the legs.

When they lifted up the body in order to let Maire see the front side, she too was shaken. The face of the body was held in a grotesque scream. Bog remnants still clung to the jawline, nostrils, and forehead; the mouth was forced wide open and filled with sod. Each tooth, though yellowed and somewhat decayed, was perfectly visible. Long reddish-blonde hair was still attached to the skull, and still in braids. A golden ball at the end of each braid glistened through the sticky damp turf. A golden torc-like necklace matched the wristlets wrapped around the corpse's right arm. The large bump in the abdominal area was the most shocking discovery. The belly pushed hard against the black plastic body bag.

The sergeant from Borrisokane was right about the body being old. He was, however, very wrong about one thing. This body was not a man's body; it was a woman's, and this woman looked pregnant.

The woman had been buried upside down in her grave, her screams for mercy left unheeded. She must have cried up until the very last moment. Begging for her life and the life of her unborn child, as the last handful of wet sod was forced into her mouth and she was lowered into her grave. Damp, cold, quicksand-like turf clung to her body and formed her sarcophagus, silencing her forever.

The crews from Limerick, Borrisokane, and Dublin, and Liam from Portumna, had beaten the heavy rain. The body was now totally wrapped in the plastic body bag, which was zippered closed and lifted by the men toward a truck that had arrived with no great fanfare, unlike the police cars and helicopter. This was a story that no one would have believed. All at the scene were visibly shaken.

Maire hard to keep from showing any emotion. “It is just the pills,” she told herself, but deep down the prospect of her own infertility and the discovery of a pregnant bog body was making her ache. Maire looked at the bulging belly and then the face.

“Who would have done this to her?” she said out loud. No one heard; they were all in a state of shock.

“We’ll need to get her to the museum as quick as we can. I’ll ride with you?” she said to the garda who brought the truck.

"The facts Ma'am, just the facts," she said beneath her breath, trying to focus on the job, not her own issues. She prided herself on her professionalism and was struggling hard to remain unemotional.

"Sergeant Joe Friday," Liam said, and waited for her to acknowledge the fact that he could accredit her quote to a TV character.

"That's it, Dragnet. Well done. Full points," she said, welcoming the distraction, and promptly continued on, "We'd better get a move on."

"Right," said Maire, turning to the crowd at the bog. "Thanks for your help, everyone. We've got to get her to Dublin as soon as possible. So we'll be hitting the road very soon." She shook hands with Liam, as she knew that he was genuinely interested in the body he had discovered.

"I'd love to know more about this whole thing," Liam said, as Maire moved away from him and grabbed her duffel bag.

"We won't know much until we do conclusive forensic testing and that could take three to six months," she said, slinging the bag over her right shoulder.

"Could I call the museum in three months to see what you have found out?" Liam persisted.
"No problem at all," said Maire, rooting through a pocket in the side of the duffel bag and handing Liam a card with her contact information.

Maire Moylan shook hands with the rest of the men and informed the two museum staff members who arrived with her via helicopter that she would be at the museum in three hours, hopefully, if traffic wasn't too bad. After refusing to consider putting the body into the helicopter, and it certainly would not have fit anyway, she was making her way to the truck. She had taken pictures of the various revelations in her excavation of the body, and would use them to carefully examine the way this body was buried. She thanked the gardaí and Liam for not calling the newspapers, but in truth no one among them had thought to.

The body, discretely covered over in the truck, was insulated with layers of damp moist sod to withstand the one-hour drive to Nenagh. A scheduled rendezvous in the parking lot of the Nenagh hospital saw the transfer of their cargo from the truck to an ambulance, providing better traveling conditions for the body, and the live people, too. It also allowed Maire to let the window down so she could cool off when the hot flashes hit and she felt like a fire-eater on a steady diet of aviation fuel. She

rode to Dublin with the window completely down, allowing the rain to splash her face.
Sergeant Hannon needed to have the last word to end the ordeal, and now that Maire was gone, he made sure of it.

“I think I can safely say our job is done here. Good luck now, Liam. Come on, Mick! Let’s head back to the barracks!”

Liam half-expected Mick O’Brien to shout, “To the bat-mobile!” Liam climbed back into the turf cutter; he threw it into reverse and shook his head in disbelief that the events of this day had ever happened at all.

“Wait until I tell the wife!” he said, “She won’t believe this one!”

Chapter 2

A wooden fence circled the Celtic island village's perimeter, high enough to stop invading tribes from climbing over it. Lough Derg was the last lake filled by the waters of the Shannon River before it flowed southwest toward Limerick and the Atlantic Ocean. There were seven huts of various sizes and one larger, long hut on the crannog.

The crannog was perfectly situated to protect its inhabitants from invaders on all sides. Celts from the northern fringes of France and Belgium had attempted to invade Ireland's southern coast in previous years. The invasions were nothing new but had become more advanced. Warrior tribes from Europe were held off at the southern shores of Ireland, but advances in their weaponry now made them far ahead of the simple Celtic tribes of Ireland, and assimilation loomed before the Irish Celts.

The Irish tribal chieftain of the crannog held meetings to inform his tribe of invasion attempts. A stone barricade protected the village from invaders by land. Sharp, jagged stones pointed threateningly away from the crannog's fence, in the direction of

all who tried to make their way onto the island dwelling, preventing invaders from making a quick advance.
The island village was surrounded by life-filled water. The water provided plenty of fish, and the woods rewarded hunters with food and fine skins to wear. The women of the tribe set up their dyeing area on the banks of the lake. Known amongst all the other tribes for the fine art of cloth dyeing, this tribe did a great deal of trade with others who longed for their brightly colored textiles. In return, they received enameled jewelry, fine pots, and cauldrons.

Children played on the banks of the lake and routinely made their way back to the village at dusk or when called. They never wandered far off into the woods, for that was where only a select few could go. They stayed near the women, who dyed the textiles, grinded grain, or cooked the meat. The animals roamed freely, along with the gods and goddesses that the tribe worshipped. Hunters and traveling druids were welcomed for their stories and tall tales.

Near the island dwelling, but toward a clearing in the forest, was the sacred spot where the Celts met for the special tribal days of Imbolc, Lunaghsa, and Samhain. Imbolc, the springtime ritual of sacrificing a lamb to the gods, was coming soon. The soft spring rain made cowslips and poppies bow their heads as if in reverence to this special time of year.

The rain washed clean the large flat rock used as an altar. This sacred place, towered over by the great spruce trees, was lit by shafts of sunlight through the luminescent shower clouds.
The tree near the altar was a ewe tree, decorated with pieces of rags tied to the branches. Each remnant of cloth, torn from a person's tunic, represented a wish: to be healed, to be loved, to give birth with ease, to have a healthy child, to live to see the next Imbolc, to become a great hunter, or to be the chieftain of the tribe.

New, young, vibrant green leaves sparkled in the shafts of light, bringing hope and the reminder that warmer weather lay ahead. The tree held promises of healing and renewing. It was a holy place for peaceful worship of the gods and goddesses of the world around them.

The air, fresh and cool, drifted like waves, filled with the flowery scents of Imbolc. The crannog was quiet. Children played with sticks, using them as swords, as the elder members of the tribe sat in the meetinghouse, discussing the successive invasion attempts by the Fir Bolgs and the Gauls on the southern shores of Ireland.
Here sat Diarmuid, the same Celt who had spared the life of a Fir Bolg warrior on the beach eight years earlier.

"This man wore the symbol of the triune goddess of birth, life, and death around his neck, just as I wore it on my wrist. We are more alike than we are different. Our strength as Celts will come from our unity as Celts, not our division."

The chieftain sat higher than the rest of the tribe, and to his right sat the red-haired Liam Ruadh, the tánaiste, and advisor to the chieftain. He was a young man but a mighty negotiator, and this was his first year as Tánaiste. Liam listened intently to Diarmuid's account of his meeting with the Fir Bolg and became agitated.

"These foreign tribes are not like us, they permit their women to fight beside them. It is the woman's role to increase tribal numbers and the man's role to defend the tribe!"

"Do we not teach our children that men and women are to coexist peacefully?" one elder asked Liam. "Are we not telling the leaders and tribal members of the future that women are life givers and men are life takers? This is inequality. Where is the peaceful coexistence we have held so sacred all along?"

Another woman asked, "We need to know how we are alike as Celts, not how different we are as tribes. This will unite us, as Diarmuid has said, and give us greater strength against the Romans, who call all Celts barbarians. "

“I have met some of the Romans who have set up a dwelling in Loughshinny,” Liam said. “Their wish to dwell on Irish soil is not troublesome to me.”

“Why?” asked the same woman.
“They are not Celts! Neither do they wish to be. They do peaceful trade with other Celtic tribes nearby. The Fir Bolgs and Gauls are more worrisome than these Roman tribes. They have a great system of government, and the women are not fighters. They serve their men better in other ways,” he said, smiling crookedly.

“The Fir Bolgs and the Gauls of the European tribes are a Celtic people, Liam! The Roman tribes are not. Their ways are not our ways,” said the woman, staring at the red-haired tánaiste.

“Maybe we should adapt to some of their ways,” Liam sneered.

“Loughshinny is just the beginning,” said Diarmuid. “Invasion does not always happen with shouting, swords, and blood. Sometimes the enemy comes and lives among us, strikes when they have befriended us!”

Grainne, the woman who had disagreed with Liam, nodded in agreement with Diarmuid and said, “I, for one, do not wish to become a slave to any man or state, Roman or Celt! Etain’s birthing day has come. I will make my way to her." With this, she stood, eyeing Liam warily. He returned her gaze with a sneering smile.

***

Etain, Diarmuid's wife, looked out toward the placid waters of the lake. This crannog had been her home for many springs and harvests. Her child was coming soon, her belly rounded and low. She had seen women die in childbirth before, and she recognized the same signs now.

A black crow perched a-top of the wooden fence of the crannog. In her thirty-three years Etain had brought life into the world seven times by seven different tribesmen, free to choose and leave her husbands as any Celtic woman was. Never before had the crow of Macha appeared to her at a birth.

The crow cawed and flew down from the wooden mast, landing on Etain's shoulder. She leaned away from it, her face turning pale. She heard the laughter of the children playing in the distance. The crow pierced its claws into her skin, stretched its wings out, and cawed again.

***

The men in the meetinghouse were silent; they knew the birthing time was near. Diarmuid in particular grew anxious, for unlike most tribal men, who could never be sure if they had fathered a particular child, he was certain that this was his wife and she would deliver his child. The sacredness of birth commanded that only other women attend her; he could not. Diarmuid had to wait until the news of his wife's and baby's health was brought to him by a woman attending the birth.

***

Grainne saw Etain slumped at the doorway of her hut with a crow perched on her shoulder, knelt at her feet, and whispered, "I dare not rid you of such an omen, Etain. This sign I have never seen before, and I do not wish to alter the course of nature."

"Grainne, if I die bringing new life, into this tribe you will remember that the child must be given the name Élan if it is a girl and Diarmuid if it is a boy." Etain's voice was weak. Her breathing was labored and heavy. Another pang of pain caused her to convulse, and her head fell back on the side of the hut when the pain subsided. The crow cawed a final time and flapped its wings. It flew off into the evergreens on the mainland.

Etain's upper body tilted to the side and slid to the floor. The baby, delivered from a dead mother, wailed healthily.

"Élan is delivered," said Grainne. She looked sadly at her friend and added reluctantly, "and so is her mother Etain. A great loss to our tribe, and to the Mother Goddess a great gain."

This child was special, born to a mother who was ushered to the underworld by the great goddess Macha in her crow-like form. When the child was cleaned they fed her from the milk of another woman, whose child had died three days earlier.

***

Etain had been a great beauty among the tribal women. Her long, golden-blonde hair and short, lean, muscular body were adored by many and enjoyed exclusively by seven tribesmen, and each of her children was fathered by a different man. All loved her deeply and respected her desire to be with another when she wanted to be. But her last husband, Diarmuid, was special to her. He wished to be with no other, and she, too, desired to be with him only.

When they first became husband and wife, Diarmuid was a young Celt, about six years younger than herself. His jet-black hair, startling blue eyes, and long, lean body made him stand out among his peers.

Their first amorous encounter was at Samhain. He watched her dance around the sparking fire, believing her to possess powers, like one of the mystical Tuatha de Dannan. Her hair glistened in the light of the fire and the full moon. Her six children, like fairies, danced sprightly behind her in glee. The braids of her hair were held at the ends by golden orbs of adornment, a gift from another husband, a blacksmith, who had mastered the art of enameling. Her fair skin was luminescent and gave her supernatural qualities. Her green eyes were expressive and soft in their gaze. She felt him watching her that night. She had watched him reach manhood. From afar, she had admired him and his slow graceful stride. He was like a lean animal roaming the wild forest, naively unafraid, unaware of any danger, yet timid and shy at the same time.

On this full moon of Samhain, when the spirits were freed from the underworld through the portals of the sidhes, the large stone doorways to and from the underworld, their eyes met across the blazing fire. The chanting and the dancing seemed to exist around them no longer. Even though she had known him since his birth, tonight he was a man and she was a woman who wanted to take him for her own, to make him her husband.

Diarmuid was nervous of this powerful woman. The men who had been with her never spoke luridly about their encounters, speaking instead of her power over them and their powerlessness in her embrace.

As effortlessly as a deer, she roamed through the gathered crowd that night. The crowd welcomed the dead spirits walking the earth freely for one night. Amidst the dancing and chanting, Diarmuid watched Etain as if she moved in slow motion, her fawn-like movements holding him rapt in attention. Etain glanced lovingly over her shoulder and spoke to her first born, Niamh.

“He stares at you, Mother,” Niamh whispered, leaning forward and pulling the long blonde hair back to whisper in Etain’s ear. Etain leant back, turning her head to see the face of her beautiful eldest child.

“Is it your desire to be with him, my love?”
“No, my eyes have fallen upon Osin,” Niamh replied, as her eyes scanned the gathering and tried to find him in the dim light.

“Then if he desires to be with me, it shall be,” said Etain. “But I will not make the pursuit an easy one. He is timid, and he needs to exert himself in order to win my affections.”

Etain had shown her daughter great reverence. Despite her own fondness for this young man, Etain would have sacrificed the relationship between Diarmuid and herself if her own daughter had desired him. By so doing, Etain would have rendered any future loving liaison between Diarmuid and herself impossible.

Across the flames, her eyes sparkled in his direction. Unmistakably, her gaze was meant for him. Her fragile lips turned upright in a tender smile. He would have to go to her. Feeling that this was much worse than the throes of a fierce hunt, Diarmuid noticed his breathing grow deliberate and his hands begin to sweat.

Slowly and purposefully, he made his way through the gathered tribe, and not once did his eyes leave her gaze. To him, it felt as if all were moving in slow motion except for himself. Her white tunic illuminated her face.

Diarmuid reached her side, his fingers clasped her hand. She felt their leanness intertwine with her fingers and encircle her wrist, a delicate touch which moved her and brought their faces together. Their foreheads touched as he leaned down to her. Her head was at the level of his chest; his great height was significant in comparison to her short stature. Even though she tilted her head back to look up into his face, he still lowered his face down to hers to allow their foreheads to touch. She closed her eyes, as did he.

All sounds ceased, except for their breathing. Her skin was cool and soft; he wanted more of it. His cheek brushed against hers, and he slid his mouth across it. His hand slid down her body, enveloping her at the waist, drawing her into him. They drew apart, and she knew he would be a beautiful lover. His thumb traced her bottom lip, she looked upward into his blue eyes, his large hands now cradling her face. She held his hand and led him from the gathering. He followed her willingly.

They crossed the crannog bridge, illuminated by burning torches tied to the larger masts. Behind them the noise of the revelry makers faded into the darkness of the October night. He held her hand and slowed his stride. They stopped on the bridge, and he pulled her to his side.

“I have been watching you for a while now,” she said, her arms sliding up his chest, around his broad shoulders, and encircling the back of his neck.

“You have?” he asked. She nodded and then kissed him.

“I have never desired another as much as I do you. You bring a calmness I have not known for many years.” His face was sincere, the eyes searching her features intensely.

Etain smiled; she knew that all warriors, like Diarmuid, were uneasy and restless souls. Killing made them this way. They walked hand in hand again toward the hut. He was different from the other men she had taken as husbands. They arrived at the opening of Etain’s hut; she led the way, still holding his hand, laughing at how low he bent to clear the door way. Inside, she began to rekindle the fire and bring it back to life, adding more dry broken branches and stoking the flames back into existence.

“Sit, Diarmuid,” she said, pointing toward a straw-filled wooden frame lined with coarse textiles.

The reviving fire threw glimpses of light on a crude table and stools. Clothes hung from twigs protruding from the wall. Beautiful ornamented bowls and a cauldron, gifts from her husband the blacksmith, who was father to her youngest child, lined a shelf to the left of the doorway. The dried flowers Etain used to treat illnesses among the tribal members decorated the walls with various colors, now muted in the dim firelight.

“What does this one do?” Diarmuid asked as he touched the clematis flower, imagining her crushing the small flower heads and making a paste with water to cure an ailment of a tribal member.

“It makes the skin itch, but it smells nice even after it has been dried,” she said, and then gave him a dried foxglove to run on his hand. “This one cures skin itch,” she said, and smiled broadly. She knew he was not knowledgeable in her methods of remedies and cures.

"Here! Rub it into your fingertips, or your skin will itch wildly," she said, extending a dried foxglove toward him.

She carried a cup of mead to him. As he took it, she held his face in her hands, and again the blue eyes startled her with their depths. She examined them more closely, tracing his eyebrows with her index finger: light blue irises with a rim of darker blue, expressive and soulful.
She ran her fingers through the thick black hair and caressed his ear. Then she kissed him on the forehead and returned to the shelf to retrieve her own cup of mead, returning then to sit beside him.

"Breathe, Diarmuid." She took an audible breath and whooshed it out. He turned to see, her hand on his knee and her face staring intently up into his. Flickers of flames were reflected in the pupils of her eyes. Her words came to him again, even more gently this time, as she moved closer.

He bent his head toward hers, their faces so close now that their lips almost touched. They kissed. He felt her hands encircle his left wrist and a leather strap touch his skin. Looking down at his arm, he watched as she tied a leather wristlet onto it. Three intertwined silver swirls on a strap of leather, the firelight glinting off the silver triune goddess symbol.

"Morrigan, Babh and Macha," she said, as she pointed to each leaf. "Birth, life, and death. Mother earth begot us all, fed us, and will envelop us at the end of our time. A warrior like you must always remember that life giving is more important and powerful than life taking. Promise me you will wear this and remember my words."

Diarmuid nodded, and Etain stretched her body up so that their eyes were now peering directly into each other's.

"Be life giving, not life taking," she whispered to him. The cups of mead, now empty, fell to the floor. He pulled her closer, into his body, and then they lay back onto the straw mattress.

For three years, they lived without their own child being born to them. Etain had delivered many children and began to wonder if she had not kept Diarmuid unfairly. The promise of having a child with him was growing increasingly uncertain. Then, in her thirty-third year, she told him her bleeding had stopped and he would be a father by the end of spring. The paternity of this child was never in doubt. This was Etain and Diarmuid's child.

When spring came and buds began to sprout small green leaves from skeletal, gray, barren branches, the earth too seemed to be celebrating the impending birth. The rivers flowed more furiously, melting snow filling them to the brim. Etain was getting ready to welcome her eighth child in May. When the pains started too early, she knew that something was wrong. Diarmuid and Etain's union was over.

***

The new born, Élan, lay cold, wrinkled, and screaming, severed from her dead mother and swaddled in Grainne's shawl.

The crying baby was carried despondently to the meetinghouse. Diarmuid rose immediately, taking the child in his arms, and then asked to see Etain. Grainne shook her head. Diarmuid stared at the child and back again at Grainne.
"Girl or boy?" he asked, in a detached tone, struggling to accept that Etain had died in childbirth.

"It is a girl, and her mother named her Élan," Grainne said.

The chieftain disbanded the others, signaling for the preparation of the body and burial of Etain. Her body was washed and dried and then dressed in her finest robes. The jewelry made for her by her husband the blacksmith was placed on her clothing. The beautiful torc of gold adorned her neck. The fibula brooch fastened her burial cloak around her neck. Her hair was braided, and the golden orbs, denoting her standing as a higher class Celt, were tied to the ends of the braids. Her skin was then brushed with finely crushed corn to even the color and keep the death look at bay until the burial. Crushed berries colored her cheeks and lips. Finally, Etain's body was placed on a burial bed of straw and wood.

All the inhabitants of the crannog returned to the hut to bid her a last farewell. The lamenting women crooned "Ochón, is Ochón O," a farewell chant.

A cauldron was filled with honey mead and carried to a large pit dug in the forest. The mead-filled cauldron was placed in a corner of the pit, her burial chamber. The dried flowers that had draped the walls of her hut now decorated the floor all around her, symbols of all she did for the tribe during her life.

At nightfall, the body, carried by the strongest men and women of the crannog, illuminated by torch bearers walking to either side, was brought to the burial chamber in the forest. The pit was now lined with more plants and flowers, emblems of what her life meant to others and how she had touched them. The men and women lowered the burial bed into the grave with straw ropes.

The mourners who carried the body knelt on the dry forest floor and used their bare hands to move the freshly dug soil into the grave and cover the body. When the grave was filled, they circled it and held hands. Again the torch bearers illuminated the inner circle of mourners by holding the torches aloft. The group looked up ward and chanted, “Protect her in the forest, Cernunnos. Lead her to the sidhes, Macha. Guide her unearthly form through the underworld, Danu. Lead her to us next Samhain.”

Diarmuid dropped to his knees, and bent his head over the ground. Etain was no longer part of his life.

In the distance, beyond the torches burning brightly on the crannog bridge, the wail of a newborn child sounded shrill and lonely on the cold spring night air.
Grainne stood holding Élan on the drawbridge. Diarmuid walked toward her hesitantly. Etain would have wanted him to remain strong, calm, and peaceful for the child. He took the baby from Grainne, and her crying softened and became a happy gurgle.

“Élan, daughter of Etain and Diarmuid, your mother has been taken to the underworld. I am your father, Diarmuid.” He kissed the baby on the forehead.

Chapter 3

Thirteen springs had come and gone since Etain's death. Élan, her daughter, had grown to be as beautiful as her mother. The best aspects of both parents were gifted to her. Like her mother, she was gentle, soft of speech, and direct and honest. Her green eyes were identical to those of Etain. The blonde locks of Etain were dark on Élan. She was muscular like both her parents, and tall like her father, though not as tall as him. She seemed older than her years, and often the men who pursued her were chased away by her father, for he was not ready to see her with a husband.

Since Etain's death, Diarmuid had grown even quieter. He conversed only with Élan, and occasionally with the chieftain of the crannog, in secret discussions with only one other person in attendance: Grainne. Élan was unaware of these meetings.

Élan had a fire within. It was as if she had outwardly inherited all the beautiful traits of her mother but inwardly housed a volcano. It lay dormant until she disliked what she saw or heard, and then the mighty hot lava of anger spewed forth in physical and verbal form. Diarmuid had seen it erupt on a few occasions, mostly in her early childhood, and usually with other children. But he himself had experience of this internal disquiet, for it was Etain who had brought his internal volcano to its dormancy. Diarmuid hoped that his daughter's internal peace would come when she found her own soul mate.

Like her mother had, Élan assisted other women during childbirth. Grainne was now the main birthing woman, but unlike Etain, she held a silent terror in her that she might do something during the birthing to hurt the mother or the child. Birthing mothers could sense Grainne's unease with her role. Élan, on the other hand, had her mother's disposition and seemed to know intrinsically that a stroking of a sweaty brow, a clasping of a clenched fist, or a soft, "Shhhh, breathe," calmed even the most anxious of birthing mothers. Because of this lovely, calming tendency in her nature, Élan became Grainne's birthing assistant. It was common knowledge amongst the tribe that Élan would be just like her mother and take her prominent place of birthing within the tribe. The women requested her presence during birthing, an her presence seemed to calm them.

Each year on the anniversary of Etain's death, Diarmuid would bring a crude wooden carving of his own face, sadness evident in its rudimentary unsmiling mouth, to a bog pool on the border of his own tribal kingdom and the next kingdom. He would tie a rock to the effigy of his own sad face and sink it into a watery, bottomless boghole. He hoped the act would take his sadness from him and send it to a never-world, neither land nor water, neither one kingdom nor another, neither air nor void, preserving it forever in the bog-land, which the Celts knew held great protective magical powers.

When his daughter Élan was old enough to comprehend the act, he would bring her with him. Both he and Élan would tie stones to wooden carvings of their sad faces and send them on an endless journey to the bowels of the earth, hoping to rid themselves of their grief. Together they would chant, "Take away our sadness at the loss of our loved one and preserve it forever in mother earth's dark place." For Diarmuid it was a cleansing act, a ritual that helped him to honor his beloved and try to move on with his life.

As Élan grew and became a young woman herself, the act of ridding himself of his sorrow became more curative. Diarmuid imagined a great void in the belly of the earth, filled with carvings of his sad face and Élan's, pulsating with his grief and sorrow of the last thirteen years.

Élan's knowledge of flowers and their healing powers also equaled and would soon surpass that of her mother. The walls of the hut she shared with her father hung heavily with foxgloves to ease skin rash, sage to improve wisdom and clarity of thinking, mugwort to help with menstrual pain, basil to promote courage, chamomile to ease stomach pain and calm nerves, patchouli to stop insects from biting, cloves to stop toothache and gossip, and lavender to heal open wounds. Élan gathered her information methodically and then retained it precisely. Even Grainne would come to her to ask advice about what to give to a child with a cough, or a woman with bad menstrual pain.

The hut smelled deliriously herbal, and despite Diarmuid's complaints of "no fresh air in here," Élan knew he was delighted that she continued her mother's gift of natural healing methods.

On nights with a full moon, when the steam from the warm moist earth stretched upward to the cool night air and wafted mysteriously toward the stars, Élan waited intently for her father to return from the gathering at the meetinghouse. Élan and Diarmuid shared a secret that no other tribal member knew. Tonight she waited a little longer than usual.

Diarmuid listened patiently to the chieftain's fears that their peaceful way of life was soon to be threatened by hostile and volatile tribes who revered the cult of the head, and not the mother goddess. As smoke filled the long house, the chieftain, the tánaiste, warriors, hunters, and women of age, drank honey mead and spoke quietly. Discussions were not rowdy affairs. Each woman and man took a turn to speak by passing a golden and ornate cup to the person with a need to speak next. They nodded to indicate agreement and waved one arm, hand out-stretched and horizontal to the torso, to indicate disagreement. Diarmuid, Grainne, and the chieftain were always the last to part ways. This was their way to meet secretly and discuss matters of great importance.

"He is like his father," the chieftain said. "He will divide the tribe with his views on the role of women."

"Chieftain," Grainne continued, "he has only one use for women, and that use destroys everything that we as a tribe revere about the mother goddess."

"I agree with his desire to prevent female warriors," the chieftain added, looking toward Diarmuid for support. "His argument is good there. If women become warriors, then who will increase tribal numbers by childbirth and heal the sick?"

Diarmuid nodded his agreement but swallowed his own guilt silently.

It was on this night that Grainne, the chieftain, and Diarmuid agreed that in five years Élan would become Chieftain and her father, Diarmuid, the Tánaiste. It was also agreed that no one would tell Liam Ruadh of his displacement until five years had passed.

Over the next five years, Élan would be trained in leadership skills and negotiation, not knowing she was being prepared for her role as tribal chieftain.

Diarmuid returned to his hut with great relief. The weight of guilt that lay heavily on him was palpable. Liberated from the tribal talks at last, he approached his hut and glanced about apprehensively to make sure that all others had returned to their own straw huts for the night.

When he stepped across the threshold, he was greeted by the illuminated green eyes searching hungrily for any indication that they were both to continue with their plans. Instead of settling into their straw beds on nights with a full moon, they both lived secret lives outside the crannog existence.

Unlike Etain, Élan could hunt. Her father relished the long, bright, full-moon nights when they would wade across the river and head for the nighttime adventures of the forests. It was under the protective shroud of nightfall that Diarmuid did something other Celtic men would never do: He taught his daughter to hunt.

Like her father, she moved stealthily through the low branches and brushed silently past the evergreen trees. Crouched low and seemingly invisible, she almost always took her prey by surprise. The animals hardly ever seemed to sense her presence in the darkness. Diarmuid gave her directions by mimicking animal sounds, and each sound meant something different. The owl's hoot meant to advance slowly, crouched low to the ground. The crow's caw meant to remain still. The whistle of a sparrow signaled the attack.

Their hunting excursions had to remain a secret, because the chieftain had long believed that women were sacred for life-giving qualities: without women the numbers of the tribe would diminish, and the tribe would lose its importance and significance amongst the clans.

The chieftain believed that tribes who had female hunters lacked the nurturing nature of clans with male hunters only. He wanted the women of his tribe to remain nurturing, to help soften the warrior ethos in the males, and to keep the delicate balance even.

A new breed of Celt had emerged, the cult of the head, made up of tribes that fought often and solved nothing. Bravado drove

these Celts to excess. The male hunters grew more fierce and began killing not only animals but also those individuals from other clans who wandered onto their hunting paths.
They killed men, beheaded them, and then scooped the brains out from cracked skulls, using the dried skulls as victory cups. The name the "cult of the head" was given to them by more peaceful clans, but it was adopted wholeheartedly by the warrior cult.

A harsh way of life without the softer female influence became disastrous. The members of the cult of the head battled within their own tribes and slaughtered without cause. Killing became an enjoyable pursuit.

The chieftain of Diarmuid's tribe met with other tribal chieftains at the October Market in Ballinasloe each year. At each gathering, he sensed that some of the tribes were becoming bloodthirsty for no apparent reason. The older chieftains who died and were replaced by younger warriors had their peaceful ways of life buried with them.

Throughout all of Ireland, there was a threat of war from abroad and within. The cult of the head had a strong hold on the majority of young warriors. Women would fight alongside their men. Death was replacing birth in importance among these tribes.

Diarmuid's tribe was self-contained, and the chieftain wanted it to remain that way, untainted by outsiders who shifted their beliefs from peaceful coexistence toward the importance of life taking.

The tánaiste, Liam, a much younger man, echoed the chieftain's words and described in detail the scenes they had both encountered at tribal markets around the island.

The tánaiste tenaciously affronted other Chieftains and Tánaistes who encouraged warrior women within their tribes. Liam Ruadh became Tánaiste because of his bravery and boldness, and his father's friendship with the chieftain. He could talk his way out of a battle better than anyone. Words were twisted and convoluted when he spoke, often baffling other people so much that they believed what he told them and not what they saw with their own eyes. A master negotiator and speaker, Liam astounded the tribe with his tales.

Liam believed he was next in line to replace the chieftain, and was a strong predecessor to execute the chieftain's wishes of no female warriors. Women in his tribe would remain revered for life giving; the added bonus of subservient females was a prospect that Liam welcomed with relish. Though Diarmuid agreed with the chieftain, and the tánaiste, the moonlight hunting excursions violated the tribal code, and he knew it all too well.

Diarmuid and Élan's secret full-moon night hunts were bitter sweet affairs. He often thought of Etain and how she was respected for her life-giving qualities. What would the beautiful Etain have thought of her daughter hunting on a moonlit night with her father?
Diarmuid convinced himself that hunting for food was far different from taking men's lives. Teaching his daughter to hunt for food was his way of teaching her to fend for herself.

They hunted under the stars and retrieved their spoils quietly. When they returned to the crannog, Élan slipped quietly into the hut, while Diarmuid hung the killed prey in the long house. Woodcock, pheasant, deer, or rabbit, Diarmuid and Élan always shared their game with the others of the tribe, but they did so anonymously. Sometimes they were so laden with animals that it took many trips back and forth across the river to bring their spoils to the crannog. Food was left in the hut and divided later among the tribal members.

Élan loved the night hunting, too. The cool air of night felt enticing on her face as she squeezed through the opening in the straw hut and stepped into the night. The crunching of the twigs, leaves, and dry moss on the forest floor beneath her feet made the tips of her fingers tingle with excitement.

When she was in pursuit of her prey, she could hear the rattling sound of the bodhran drum playing a methodical fast beat in her head, beating a rhythm to match the pace of the rabbit, deer or whatever else she hunted. The night was more alive to her than the day. She loved how the full moon threw beams of light through the trees, playing games with her vision, forcing her to sharpen her wits and her eyesight, making the hunt even more fun and challenging, the way she liked it. She hunted well, but not as well as her father.

On this night, three pheasants, four rabbits, and a woodcock had fallen with arrows through their bodies. Father and daughter loaded their hoard and found their way through the dark forest back to the crannog.

Élan squeezed herself between the upward-facing drawbridge and the fence of the crannog. She took each animal from her father and laid it on the crannog floor beside her. Diarmuid pulled himself up from the river and squeezed himself into the narrow opening between the drawbridge and the fence. He saw the dead animals lying on the ground, he saw Élan's smiling face, and behind her he saw human feet.

His eyes slowly traveled upward to the ankles, knees, hips, torso, shoulders, and face. Water dripped from Diarmuid's body as he pulled himself to standing on the crannog floor. Élan saw the change in his face and followed his stare. She turned to see what held her father's gaze. They came face to face with Liam Ruadh, the tánaiste.

Liam seemed puzzled at the events unfolding before his eyes. He was a younger man than Diarmuid, but only by about four years. Both men knew that this was indeed a very tricky, very delicate situation. Liam, the strong negotiator, would strike a bargain tonight that would serve him well.

"Moonlight hunting, Diarmuid?" The voice was filled with a smooth tone of gratification.

Diarmuid nodded. This was not a good situation for his daughter or himself, and he was fully aware of it.

"Are you cold, Élan?" Liam asked gently, as he turned toward her. His hand lay gently on her shoulder. Instinctively, Diarmuid wanted to rip it away, sensing that Liam's motive was lurid.

"No, Tánaiste, just my feet are cold." Her answer was soft and honest.

He took in her features as she answered and congratulated himself silently on securing his future with such a beautiful creature.

"Because they are wet?" His hand slid down her arm and brushed her skin. Élan was unsure of what was happening, but she knew that she felt uncomfortable in the Tánaiste's presence.

"Yes," Élan said, her green eyes elucidated by the light of the full moon. Her skin seemed luminescent in the night, and Liam nodded knowingly at her. She would be his prize for this night's illicit goings-on.

Teaching a woman to hunt was a great crime. Liam, happy he had discovered them, would now negotiate a handsome deal for himself. Beautiful Élan would be his wife. She would take him and only him and they would be exclusive to each other. She would serve him and only him, all of her life. His gaze, lasting a moment too long, made her step backward, freeing herself from his touch.

Élan felt awkward under his stare and looked toward her father. Diarmuid knew Liam's gaze all too well. Élan was an object of desire. Liam Ruadh's lips bowed upward, and his crooked smile broadened, eventually baring his yellowing teeth.

"It would be best for you to return to the hut. You will fall sick." Liam spoke to Élan directly and softly. He stepped toward her and commenced caressing her arm. Diarmuid restrained himself from grabbing the Tánaiste by the throat and choking him.

Élan looked at her father for approval; he gave it by nodding slowly. Diarmuid waited for his reprimand and silently thanked the mother goddess that Élan was free to leave.

"Goodnight, Élan," Liam said, as he turned to watch her walk away, taking in every sway of her body, every movement of her form. He did not hide his lurid gaze from Diarmuid.

When she was no longer in view, Liam turned back again to face Diarmuid.

"You brought her hunting with you, Diarmuid? After all of our talks in the meetinghouse about not educating women in the ways of hunting?"

"It is a sport we both enjoy." Diarmuid's response was sharp.

"It defies the ruling against women being warriors. Were you not at the meeting when the chieftain spoke at length about this matter?" This was spit out sadistically, but Liam knew he had Diarmuid right where he wanted him.

"Women who hunt for food are not warriors, they are hunters," Diarmuid said, as he bent to retrieve the dead animals.

Liam bent down to meet his eyes. He clasped his hand over Diarmuid's hand, and their eyes fixed on each other.

"Women who are hunters are taught to kill. Women who are hunters are killers. They lose their nurturing ways." Liam had the upper hand, and they both knew it.

"Élan would never use her hunting knowledge on a person." Diarmuid's plea bargain for his daughter was failing; he lacked the negotiating skills of Liam Ruadh.

Liam nodded, but not in agreement. His nod was from internal knowledge that he was going to win this argument easily. "This does not change what I have seen here tonight Diarmuid. You have directly disobeyed the ruling of the Chieftain of this tribe."

"Élan is a good woman. I will not bring her hunting anymore. Let us not speak of it again?" Diarmuid said softly, he knew this was a delicate topic, that he and Élan were indeed guilty and had broken a tribal ruling. He knew it was time to beg.

"Liam, this is our only home. Think with your heart before you make your decision."

Liam saw his chance, and he grabbed it. The deal would be struck this night and adhered to until she became his wife and he owned her. He had Diarmuid right in the palm of his hand, and it felt good. Liam stood up slowly.
"The chieftain and elders will never know of this night's events Diarmuid."

"Thank you, Liam," came the response, but inwardly Diarmuid knew there was a stipulation to follow. Again the two men were caught in each other's stare.
"I ask only one thing of you in return for my silence to protect you and Élan."

"What is it you ask of me, Liam?"

"Élan will be mine in five years, and we will never speak of this night to the chieftain." The crooked, self-satisfied smile returned to Liam's lips.

“Élan is a free woman. Free to choose husbands,” Diarmuid said, slinging the dead animals over his shoulder.

“My silence about tonight’s events in return for Élan at eighteen years.” Liam’s voice was now low, deliberate, and threatening.

“I cannot promise you what is not mine!” Diarmuid said, forcing the words to remain calm as they came out of his mouth, though inwardly he was screaming. The thought of Élan imprisoned by this conniving animal of a man filled him with contempt.

“Then I cannot promise either of you my protection tonight. I must reveal to the tribal members the events of this night, come morning.”

“The chieftain will warn us, and there will be nothing more to it. Of that I am sure!” said Diarmuid now turning away in the direction of the long house.

“The chieftain will turn you out of the crannog and leave you at the mercy of the cult of the head. The chieftain will believe what his tánaiste tells him, of that you can be certain. You are also aware that I myself will be chieftain one day, probably very soon,” said Liam, wiping his hands on the side of his tunic. He tilted his head to one side and smiled.

"My silence for Élan?" he repeated.

Knowing the secret, that Liam would never be chieftain, gave Diarmuid courage. The great secret that in five years Élan would be chieftain, and he tánaiste, was Diarmuid's single calming thought.

Despite the fact that Élan was not his to give, that night, under the full moon that illuminated the crannog between drifting silvery clouds, he gave his daughter away. Diarmuid made a mock deal, secure in the knowledge imparted to him by the current chieftain and Grainne, that Liam Ruadh would never be the tribe's chieftain.

The nights of moonlit hunts were over, and though Élan would beg and plead him to take her hunting, he knew that he could never share the hunt with her again.

"No more hunting with her," came the words from behind him as he made his way across the crannog to the hut. Diarmuid stopped halfway between Liam and the opening to his hut. He turned to look at Liam.

"Five years from now," Liam reminded him, and then walked away.

Diarmuid was left to ponder the deal he had struck that night. He could only hope that the chieftain lived for the next five years and that his daughter would then rule the tribe.

***

On the southern tip of Ireland, foreign tribes were sailing ashore. With them, they brought new warrior tactics and weapons. The response to change became to accept the change itself. No native tribe could over-power the foreign tribes.

The Fir Bolgs had made their way across the Irish Sea from Belgium and discovered a way of life that they could adapt to easily in Ireland. The Fir Bolgs were mighty horsemen with hair styled high on their heads, brandishing swords from a-top their horses. Their women rode beside them, warriors also, and as fierce as the men.

This Celtic tribe had learned to fend off many other warrior tribes in Europe, each battle making them stronger and teaching them to learn from their previous mistakes.

By the time they had migrated to Ireland, their spear heads were no longer stone or bone. The art of using molten iron ore had been perfected, and iron shields, swords, and spear-heads bolstered their tactics and conquests. Their efforts at warfare and conquering had reinforced them so greatly that by the time they moved northward from the southern coast of Ireland toward Tipperary and Meath, the native tribes, though ready for the battle, were no match for the Fir Bolgs.

The men of the local tuatha fought bravely against these mighty horsemen. Yelling madly, they ran naked into battle, the cry of the Celts echoing throughout forests and over hillsides, and they met their death quickly. The Irish Celts lacked the weaponry and the horsemanship of their European foes.

Fir Bolg women, too, with hair whitened and berry juice on their nails and hands to stain them red, barraged the battle fields of Celtic Ireland with the same prowess and vigor as the males. They fought alongside their men and died alongside them, too.

The crannogs were taken over effortlessly once the warriors were disposed of. Elders were killed, and native women and children were assimilated with little effort into the Fir Bolg tribe.

Two years after invading the southern coast of Ireland, the Fir Bolg tribes had moved northward and had taken dals, tribal lands, and crannogs for their own. The assimilation of Irish Celts into Belgae Celts was a bloody, war-filled, and aggressive transition.

Though both groups were Celtic, and shared many common characteristics, the role of women within the tribes divided them. From the assimilation of Irish and Belgae Celts, new customs and beliefs were born. It was a time of great fear and trepidation for native Irish Celts, who knew that their way of life was soon to be crushed. The cult of the mother goddess was being replaced by the cult of the head.

***

Diarmuid's tribe remained hidden and safe until the first snows of winter. It would take the Fir Bolgs two years to find the crannog on a small inlet of water on the northern shores of Lough Derg. But find it they did.

They came on horseback, wearing ornate cloaks and carrying intricately decorated shields. The harnesses of the horses were embellished with colorful stones, and the breath of man and horse was exhaled like a powerful mist of poison, tainting the cold winter air. Stealthily and carefully, they picked their way along the safe hunting paths, closing in on the crannog and its inhabitants. Broken branches, pieces of fur, and animal skins, all telltale signs left by previous hunters, led the Fir Bolg directly to Diarmuid's tribe.

It had been four years since Diarmuid had given his consent to Liam that Élan would be his. When he told her of the events of that night, she cried. Despite his assurances that Liam would never be chieftain and that she would never have to be his wife, Élan lived in fear of it.

As her eighteenth year approached, she imagined that she would escape and live in another crannog, free to make her own choice of husbands. But she stayed with her father and marked the number of moon cycles until her eighteenth year on an ogham stone in the forest. She had one more moon cycle remaining.

Élan sat carving a line through a circle on the ogham stone when she heard the sound of a large grunt in the distance. Hiding low, between the evergreen trees and the skeletal branches of leafless winter trees, she saw them coming.

The sound of the horses' hooves hitting the hard, cold forest floor and crunching through dead leaves, dried pine needles, and snow made her body shiver. The closer they came, the more the ground pulsed. She curled herself up in a ball and hid beneath the low, canopy-like branches of the spruce tree beside her. Despite her great effort to be quite and breathe as silently as possible, she felt that each frosty breath was beckoning them in her direction.

When the hoof beats had trailed off into the distance, she realized that they were heading toward the crannog. She understood that she was safe, but the others were not. It was then that she felt a great fear of loss. She knew intrinsically that these were the dreaded Fir Bolgs.

Her nostrils flared and her heart beat quickened, and unable to control her emotions, she ran toward the crannog, tears streaming down her cheeks. Her father, she needed to be with him now.

The dense smell of musk was strong on the wind. The cold air moved heavily and powerfully between the huts on the crannog. Like a powerful, cruel animal, the winds of winter prowled around the huts, lurking coldly around the doors. The cold mist, swirled and preyed, animal-like, stalking its victim in silence. This winter was going to be cold and long, a winter full of change.

It was shortly before the winter solstice when the Fir Bolgs made their way across the drawbridge, with the women, children, and men of the tribe staring blankly at the fierce warrior tribe before them. Their assimilation seemed inevitable.

The warriors a-top of their horses were adorned in clothing and weaponry that the crannog clan had never seen before. In the early days of winter, as snow shone on the straw roof-tops and fence of the village, the Fir Bolgs did something unusual for warrior tribes. They did nothing. There was no fierce battle. The Fir Bolg entered the crannog with authority and power. They had the upper hand.

The leader was a man with white hair, tied in a strange knot to the left side of his head. He wore a great leather cloak lined at the edges with animal fur. His men, sitting straight on their steeds behind him, scanned the crannog in silence. This would be an easy take over. The great leader, showing no fear, also admired the view of the crannog from the top of his horse. He smiled, his fierce blue eyes penetrating the entire crowd. His broad shoulders moved upward as he sat even higher on the horse and commanded the animal to lower its head, which it did immediately.

"Bring your chieftain to me," boomed the voice of this man, their tallest and most ornately adorned warrior. His words were coated with an accent from mainland Europe. Though he spoke the language of Ireland, it was affected with his accent. Yet the crowd standing before him understood the order.

The chieftain walked slowly, assisted by his wife, from the back of the crowd, and parted with her to stand alone in front of this tall imposing warrior.

“I am this crannog’s chieftain,” he said, in a voice that he wanted to sound strong and powerful but instead came out old and weak. He moved uneasily to the side of the warrior’s horse and held onto its reins for support.

A strange implement was lifted from the warrior’s side. He brandished it aloft in the air, and it shone and glimmered beautifully in the watery winter sunlight, as it swiftly came down across the left shoulder of the chieftain and severed his head and shoulders at a sloping angle from his body. The action was so swift and silent that the crannog tribe was unaware of what had happened. Never before had they seen a sword.

So swift was the action that the chieftain did not scream in pain. His head and shoulders slipped away from his body, which stood momentarily and then buckled at the knees and dropped. Blood flooded the area. People screamed, and the warrior’s voice boomed loudly above the din of panic. No one heard him speak.

The inhabitants of the crannog continued to scream. The men moved forward, chests pushed out, and voices loud and angry. From either side of this fearsome warrior the other men moved toward the crowd, horses grunting and filling the crannog air with their wintery, steamy breaths. Women held onto their men and used their cloaks to shield the eyes of their children.

“Silence!” The warrior lifted the blood-stained sword above his head. “I am your chieftain now,” he said, and then turned when he heard the clatter of feet running across the wooden bridge.

Élan’s feet pounded heavily on the drawbridge and resounded in the dead silence of the crannog. The horses and warriors stirred uneasily when they sensed another presence behind them. They parted the way and allowed her to pass through. She saw the chieftain’s body cut in two and drenched in blood on the ground. Her hands immediately lifted to her mouth, and she screamed. The tears flooded her eyes involuntarily, and she looked up at the warrior with the blood-stained sword. His piercing blue eyes seemed devoid of emotion, while her green eyes were overflowing with it. She began pounding on his leg and the horse’s side violently.

“Amach! Amach! Amach!” she yelled, through screams and boiling hot tears, the volcano in her chest erupting and spewing forth without her control.
Diarmuid and Liam both yelled her name simultaneously, as the warrior leapt from his horse and grabbed her by the arms. Her head was to his chest. The strength in his arms was inhuman. He could easily have crushed her bones if he had tightened his grip, but he didn’t.

“What does Amach mean?” he said, as she continued to cry and then began to kick him. Losing her breath and then screaming again, she continued, the uncontrollable emotions pouring forth. But her blows were like that of an ant on a lion. The other warriors laughed heartily at her bravery and endurance.

Again he asked, through laughter, “Come now, tell me the meaning of Amach.”

She stopped kicking and crying and gritted her teeth. She turned her face upward toward his and spit at him. This time he did not laugh.

“It means, GET OUT!” she said, her breath uneven and heavy.

He let go of her arm and leaned his body weight onto his blood-stained sword, which now stuck in the ground beside him. He took a closer look at his assailant.

Dark curly hair that draped across her shoulders and down her back, burning green eyes that would have killed him if they could, nostrils flaring like that of a horse in high gallop. Her chest heaving with heavy breaths and her rosy freckled cheeks stained with tears.

“I am here to stay,” he said, smiling. “If I go, though, I promise you that you will come with me. We will both be ‘Amach,’” he said, and he laughed, joined by other warriors near them.

Chapter 4

When people first met Maire, they were intrigued by her line of work. The question that everyone asked her was how she got into the field of forensic archaeology. Her answer was always the same. When she was a girl, her favorite story from the Irish legends was the Children of Lir, and *Forensic Files*, was her favorite television show.

Moylan was the oldest of four children. The other three, all boys, toughened her up with wrestling matches, dares, and the odd threat of “We’ll tell Mammy!”

Despite the odd bruise or scratch, she enjoyed her brothers. She was one tough girl at soccer and her brains would out match her brothers’ brawn any day.

There was a long period of friendly academic competition that served her well when secondary school came to an end. The days of dissecting frogs, dead cats, and mice on the farm gave her an interest in biology and science that far outlived her brothers’ interest in it.

She graduated top of her class at Trinity, and then veered into her career in forensic archaeology because of a two-week summer holiday in New York. It was there that she saw an American show, *Forensic Files*, which demonstrated how a strand of yarn found in a car linked a six-year-old murder victim wearing a Wal-Mart Sesame Street sweater to her murderer, eight years later. That was it, Maire was hooked.

It was like being Sherlock Holmes in the age of microbes and microscopes. Science solved the murder, eight years later. She was immediately drawn to the field of forensics. Moylan never looked back on her choice of career. It was relatively new in Ireland and she was sought after night and day.

Maire's knowledge and skills in the field were renowned throughout museums and the homicide unit in each major city's gardaí barracks. She was a bit of an enigma among the boys in the business. Having grown up on a cattle farm, she was no stranger to blood and gore and hard work for long hours. It was nothing for her to carry great lumps of cows' afterbirth to the trash heap. Not to mention living through the torment, lovable though it might have been, of sharing a house with three younger brothers. She was just one of the boys at home, and now again at work.

Maire Moylan was impervious to the comments and under-the-breath innuendos that greeted her on crime scenes. She loved her work, and what anyone else said or thought just didn't matter.

Maire's mother had gifted her a cook-book, kitchen knives, an ironing board and iron, aprons, toasters, and more cook-books for every birthday and Christmas that Maire could remember. Finally, she gave in and asked Maire, "When are ye going to have a baby, for God's sake?" Not too soon, Maire hoped, but now the prescription pills to help her get pregnant might change her plans.

Rory wanted a family badly; Maire wasn't in as much of a rush. To her mother's chagrin, Maire would definitely never be the Calor Cosingas House-wife of the Year. Maire would, however, excel in a world that was dominated by men, the world of forensic archaeology. It was a happy choice that had led her to great heights in her profession. But with two great disappointments to her mother—, a traditionally male career and still no babies, after three years of marriage!

Maire had graduated with a degree in forensic archaeology from Trinity College Dublin in 1991, and she developed such an interest in the Iron Age that she continued on to pursue a Master's degree, and eventually started her doctoral study researching why bogs were chosen as burial sites for Iron Age people.

Her theories so far were based mostly on supposition, and, despite the fact that she had been called to exhume two other partial remains of bog bodies, she still needed factual evidence to back her theories. Her doctorate remained unfinished despite a backload of evidence from Roman writers during Iron Age times; she still couldn't prove that bogs were deliberately chosen for specific reasons to bury people during the Iron Age.

Maire wanted so desperately to prove that the Celts were trapping the souls of perpetrators in a world of "betweens" — between the land and the water, for bog-land was both, and it was neither. This was an impossible task because the Celts had no written language. Their tongue remained oral only, and they would develop a crude form of written communication later, when they wrote on ogham stones with markings to show the passing of days or seasons, no words were ever passed down through written means.

Still, she had secured a job at the National Museum and was glad of it. She began a post as a forensic archaeologist at the museum leaving her professorship at Trinity College Dublin in 1997. She was now into her seventh year at the museum. Seven years, and still no end in sight for the abandoned ideas of her doctorate. The push to have a child became even stronger when her husband Rory used this fact against her.

"Sure, you are at a standstill with your Ph.D.? Now's the time, Maire! Strike while the iron is hot!" He grabbed her from behind and pulled her into him, kissing the back of her neck and her shoulders.

"Are ya sure it isn't yourself that's hot there?" she joked. But lately, the jokes were not diverting him from the prospect of having a family, and soon.

***

In the journey from the bog back to the museum in Dublin, the effects of the prescription pills had waxed and waned all the way across the country, in what Maire thought was the second-worst ride of her life. The ride in the helicopter earlier in the day took first place, easily. If the effects of the pregnancy were going to be as bad as the effects of the prescription pills, and she was only a few weeks into the deal here, Maire was not too crazy about the prospect of feeling this way for nine months.

Maire had arranged for two museum people to wait at the lab door and help with the bog body. The two people, a man and a woman, pushed the stretcher over to the truck's tailgate before the truck had even pulled to a full stop. The body was carefully lifted out, and Maire Moylan began chanting, "Easy does it now! Easy does it!"

Soon this body would begin to reveal its' story to her. She was anxious to learn that story. Forensics was like reading a good book. The next chapter helped you to make guesses as to how the book would end. Maire could barely wait to start the Carbon-14 tests. Then the paleodietary testing would follow. The tests would reveal how old the woman was, what her diet consisted of, how she died, what time of year she died, and possibly why she was buried in such a manner. The hardest part for Moylan was waiting for the results of each test. The investigation could take months to come to a conclusion. Lost in her own thoughts of what this bog body would reveal, Maire felt the stretcher bump against the concrete parking lot toward the ramp entrance to the museum forensics lab. The stretcher jolted and jarred against the ramp.

The museum staff in forensic archaeology couldn't wait to see the state of the body. Sometimes their anticipation over took their respect for the dead bodies in the museum. Maire tried hard to respect the fact that bog bodies were still *bodies*. They had been people who died possibly brutal, agonizing deaths, and they needed to be treated with respect. The bog bodies, she believed, brought them face to face with long-lost ancient ancestors.

"Slowly now," said Maire, as the gurney's legs were lifted the half inch up to the ramp as the two guards, Maire, and the museum staff members made their way to the medical examiner's office. The door was immediately thrown open, and a large blonde man stepped outside. All silence was broken. The man was whistling, "Please release me, let me go" and realizing how appropriate the song was for the scene unfolding before him, he burst into flamboyant theatrics, spreading his arms out and leaning back to belt out the first few lines again.

"Please release me, let me go, For I don't love you anymore!"

The two museum staffers laughed, but the two gardaí that accompanied Maire in the truck from the bog in Tipperary looked at each other in disbelief.

"Tis all right men," came the mock military drawl with a hint of County Kerry. "We'll take it from here."

Immediately he tried to unzip the body bag.

"What have you got for me darling?" he said, in a rich, lilting Kerry accent, as he placed his hand on Maire's shoulder.

"A kick in the balls if you think that this one is yours." She slapped his hand off the body bag, redoing the zip back up.

“Hands off, you lazy bastard, I answered the call first. So this one belongs to me.”

By this time, both gardaí had abandoned their pushing of the stretcher and realized they were on foreign soil. They took turns shaking hands with Moylan; she thanked them again for their help. Their shoes clipped sharply on the shiny blue linoleum, one garda shook his head at what seemed to be a lack of professionalism on behalf of the Kerry man in the lab coat.

“Don’t go! I was just about to make espresso!” came the Kerry lilt again.

“You are a right character, Sullivan,” said one of the museum workers.

“Did ye ever see Young Frankenstein lads? Ah! It’s a very funny film!”

“Let’s go, Sean!,” said Maire, her patience already wearing to a thin veneer, and pointing at the black body bag on the stretcher.

“There is the possibility that you might find this even more interesting than Young Frankenstein,” she added, with mock enthusiasm for Sean’s benefit.

“Ah now, don’t be greedy. You have to share me with other people, too,” said Sean, as he eyed the body bag up and down.

There was no doubt about it, Sullivan was a pain in the arse at the best and the worst of times, but he knew his stuff when it came to Celtic history and forensic archaeology. Sometimes he could make you laugh out loud, but there were times when he just didn’t know when to turn it off. Then again, he could get so super-focused on something that everything else was shut out, and he saw or heard nothing, only the object that had captured his attention. Maire knew that this bog body would do that to Sullivan. She was secretly glad he was here.

Sean was a serial dater, a man with every intention to bed and no intention to wed. Maire imagined him marrying in his mid to late fifties after having squired half the young women in the country. He would only marry, she believed, when he got too old and curmudgeon-like to endure a new woman every weekend and have to fake the interested-chap lark and turn on the charm. He was very much the type of lad she wouldn’t have touched with a forty-foot barge pole when she herself was in the dating world. Yet, here she was, spending nine to five with him five days a week. She saw more of Sean than she did of her husband Rory.

"Thanks, lads, we'll take it from here," said Moylan to the two museum workers. Her arm embraced the frame of the stretcher, forcing them to let go of it. They stood upright and still. They watched the stretcher and the three people, Maire, Sean Sullivan, and the bog body— disappear inside the door

Sean held the door open as Maire negotiated the gurney through the entrance way. A few bumps against the door-frame, and they were in the next hallway. The gurney rolled more easily on the blue linoleum. Maire felt relieved that the woman's body was safely at its destination. The double doors closed behind them. The gurney's wheels screeched as they rolled down the hallway.

"Right!" said Maire, with a triumphant flair.

"Come on now, *Mrs.* Moylan!" Sean stressed the "Mrs." He loved to attribute an older woman's persona to Maire, although she was two years younger than him.

"Share the wealth. What lies beneath this body bag? Give us a quick look, will ya?" he said, trying to unzip the bag; again, the slap and harsh reminder.

"Well, if you got your arse out of bed and to work on time you might not have to beg for a piece of the action. Where were you this morning anyway?" Maire said, as she steered the gurney down the hallway.

"Myself and Jim went to Judge Roy Beans. Met a couple of yanks who wanted us to show them the town, you know?" Sean smiled at her agitated yet interested look.

"I do now. Did you forget to go home or what?"

"No, by God! I slept in splendor at Jury's Hotel last night. I had to go home and shower and change before work. Is that all right Mammy?"

Maire hated this. He knew that she disliked being called "Mammy" just by watching her eyebrows knit together and the "11" wrinkle appearing between them.

"You are a woeful shite, Sean Sullivan! You can take a look so long as you know that this is my case and you are my assistant on it. Deal or no deal?" she said, seeing that he now was totally perplexed about what was transpiring before him. She knew that the minute he saw the dress and the hair, he would be in shock.

"Deal," he said, with a hint of uncertainty that he had indeed struck a good bargain. He felt quite certain that he had made a good deal when she unzipped the body bag slightly to reveal the upper torso of the body.

Despite the clumps of moist peat clinging to the body, parts of the dress, hair, and facial features were distinctly visible through the mess. Shimmers of the golden torc around the body's neck gleamed in the stark fluorescent lighting. Sullivan touched the torc lightly and his lower lip fell open in a gawp of amazement. This had to be the most perfect find for a bog body, ever.

Sean Sullivan's face went white. The tragedy of her burial was not yet known to him, but the ornate dress and hair decorations immediately aroused his curiosity, and he *was* glad he had made the deal with Maire.

"Don't say a word yet." Maire's hushed and secretive voice brought him back to reality.

"Why?" Sullivan asked, looking up at her, but his mind was far away and his brow creased with a cavernous furrow.

"Because there are some pictures you need to see. Sign in receipt of delivery, and then we'll talk."

"The burial site?" he inquired.

"Not your typical burial, I would have to say," Moylan added. "There is more to this than meets the eye, Sean, believe me. Now go and get the paperwork signed," she added.

Sullivan couldn't wait. He was off like a greyhound.

"Put her in the drink first, but remove the clothing!" he said. "I'll get everything ready for the examination. Careful with the clothes now! Careful!" The Kerry lilt was no longer jovial, but high pitched and focused; Sean was in work mode.

"Do ya think I'm some sort of ejit, Sullivan? How the hell did I survive before you came along? Ya gobshite," Maire thought to herself as she laboriously pushed the gurney along the "so shiny you might slip" insipid blue linoleum. The wheels screamed for a lubricant of any sort to take them out of their misery, the noise itself so loud it echoed through the hollow hall.

"Stop crying, my love, I'll be there in a minute!" Sean yelled back along the hallway in the direction of the screeching gurney. The ambulance driver looked puzzled at Sean.

"When I win the lotto, I will buy enough WD40 to oil every wheel on every gurney we own here," Sean said, and added with pseudo solemnity, "We have two gurneys."

Not getting the reaction he desired from the driver, he continued on. “That makes *eight* wheels!” He beamed a fake smile that made the Hollywood sign look dull. The driver blurted out a giggle. Sean, pleased that he had broken the mood and finally gotten a laugh, scribbled his illegible signature on the receipt.

Maire pushed the gurney along the corridor and turned left into the examination room. Popping her head out into the hallway again, she heard the muffled laughter and became impatient.

“Come on, Sean!”

“Cool, calm, and collected darling!” he sang back in his lilt, but she could tell that Sean was as eager as she was to get to work on this bog body.

“Yeah! Yeah!” she mumbled, as she maneuvered the stretcher beneath the lights, a stark bright reality in contrast to the surreal events of the day.

“Keep a cool head, and dry pants!” She droned automatically, her eyes roaming the full length of the bog body.

“A tribal queen perhaps?” she imagined.

She crossed the room and began washing her hands at the sink. In the stillness of the room, the voice of Sean Sullivan singing “Please Release Me” snipped the air like cutting shears.

The water felt cool and refreshing on her hands. She bent over and splashed her face. Then she methodically soaped up and dried her hands, and pulled on a pair of insipid-green Touch ‘n’ Tough latex gloves. Turning to face the plastic-covered body, she grabbed the apron hanging on the hook behind the closet door, tying it as she ambled toward the lifeless, formless mound of plastic resting on the gurney.

“Let’s begin, shall we?” Maire said to her lifeless guest, in a mockingly polite tone, as she flexed her fingers and clenched and unclenched both fists. Her stomach gave a little queasy jump, and she rested her hands on either side of the gurney frame. Maire looked up and closed her eyes. Hopefully the symptoms of the pills wouldn’t get worse. She hadn’t eaten since breakfast, and even that was just dry toast and a cup of tea. A couple of deep breaths later, and the sensation had passed. She loosened up her shoulders with a slight wiggle and placed her hands a-top of the plastic body bag.

Maire unzipped the bag slowly to reveal the upper torso area only. Bits of bog were now caught in the zipper, so it took a few attempts to unzip completely. Up and down, up and down, back and forth went the zipper as she tried to loosen bog bits and peat particles from its teeth. Her impatience grew steadily worse.

“Fuck it,” as she attempted to unzip again, it stopped dead. “Shit,” her second attempt failed to pass the same point. “Come on ya bastard!” The language had become absolutely beautiful since the introduction of the ‘get pregnant pills,’ and patience with inanimate objects was no longer a virtue she possessed. Patience with people was a close second. “Third time is the charm,” she growled between gritted teeth, and the zipper passed the point of being stuck and its teeth parted easily around the rest of the bag.
As it gave way, she folded the body bag over the chest to reveal only the face and shoulders for now. Her heart beat quickened, and her palms became a bit sweaty.

Beneath the bright operating lights the remarkable skin and features were clearly visible. With a very soft bristled brush, Maire began to brush away the remaining pieces of peat and sod. It was only when she began to remove the clumps from the mouth that she began to feel deep sorrow for the woman. The beautiful features, hair, and clothing, all were marred by the horrifying shape of the mouth as it was forced open in its eternal scream by the sod inside.

The peat seemed to have been forced into the mouth. The cavity was stuffed to the bursting point. The tongue, stiffened by rigor mortis, pushed hard to one side as the mouth cavity was cleared of all peat. Still the eternal scream held its shape. The eyelids were closed, caked with dried peat. Maire dusted the peat particles away from the inside corners of the eyes and across the eyelids and brows. Dark brown lashes and eye brows slowly revealed themselves. The eyelids were so supple that she couldn't resist the urge to take hold of the lash and lift the lid open. She hesitated when reaching for the eye-lashes, fearing that she would rip them from the flesh. Instead, she turned to a table behind her and retrieved a small implement like a blunt spatula, only smaller. She turned toward the body. Moylan slowly wedged the implement gently between the upper and lower lashes.

The flesh was so supple that the lid easily lifted open and there beneath the creased upper lid, now folded back like a curtain drawn aside to reveal the interior, was an empty socket. Maire stepped back and dropped her arms to her sides, relieved that there was no eyeball staring back at her. Again the spatula-like implement lifted the left eye lid open to reveal a cavity of bone and dirt.

Around the neck, beneath the beautiful reddish-brown braids and the cloak, was a golden torc which looked as if it had been twisted even tighter around the neck to choke the woman. The bands of gold were woven around each other, and the ends of the torc had the typical curvilinear details of Celtic jewelry already on display in the museum. Lines and curves, with no visible beginnings or endings, swirled around in a maze.

The details of the torc, when dusted clear of dried peat, revealed a deer's head on either end, with leaves and flowers. Again this was typical Celtic imagery. When Maire eased the torc away from the neck, she saw that the skin had been indented permanently with the spirals and twirls of the torc's designs. One of the deer heads had left its indentation permanently on the neck of the woman.

Maire stood back and took a deep breath. Hopefully this body would leave forensic science the clues and hints needed to determine the cause of death. It certainly looked as if the clues were already there; testing of course, would be more conclusive.

Again Maire reached into the oral cavity to satisfy a curiosity. As she turned her head briefly, she thought that she saw something glisten from the back of the corpse's throat. Turf again became dislodged as Maire rooted deeper into the back of the oral cavity. There was definitely something golden in the corpse's throat.

"Well, how does she look?" bellowed Sean, as he sauntered across the room.

The sight of Maire pulling bits of turf out of the body's mouth made him guffaw in delight, "You can take the woman out of the bog, but you can't take the bog out of the woman," he cheered. Maire lifted her head slowly and turned toward Sean. She was not amused.

"It is a wonder that any woman would want to spend a minute with you, never mind an entire night."
"I don't mean to toot my own horn or anything, but rumor has it that I am great in the old sack. You know?"

"Keep hitting on married women behind their husbands' backs, and rumor has it you'll be great in a body bag, ya ejit!" Maire replied dryly, shaking her head in disbelief at Sean's bravado. "God almighty, Sean, have you ever heard of decorum?"

"No. Is she good looking?" was the reply.

Sean could handle a leathery, dried-up and wrinkled to the point of "Is it a human or a saddle bag?" type of bog body. This bog body was like a fairly recently buried corpse. It made him uneasy.

The relationship between Maire and Sean was not at all strained. Neither pretended to be something that they were not. She was genuinely uninterested in him and his chauvinism, and likewise, he was not interested in her and her feminism. Both were respectful of each other's knowledge in their own specific fields. Though she would never admit it to Sean, there had been many a day when his humor had lifted her spirits after a fight with Rory at home had remained unresolved.

It was liberating, in a way, to know that you could be offensive and not offend. In truth, Maire was intimidated by Sean's self-proclaimed libido and prowess. She was too drained to even talk sex with her husband most nights, let alone engage in it. Rory and she were now in the passionate throngs of "Are you ovulating yet? Should we have a go then, or what?" Most of the time she wanted to respond, "Or what?" but Rory's determination to become a father had replaced his ability to detect mockery. Sean, on the other hand, seemingly never tired of the act, or the talk of sex.

It was the lighthearted way that Sean talked about sex that was liberating. Then again, he didn't have to go home and cook dinner each night and run a household and try to get pregnant, even though you weren't quite sure it was what you wanted, but you were certain it was what your husband wanted. Hell!

Judging by the greeting she got at her home-place for Christmas, it was what everyone wanted, except Maire.

“Yearra, come on now, you love the attention. Tell me how much ya love me!” Sean said, as he made his way to the side of the stretcher.

“Lord, you are a woeful gobshite Sean.” She giggled and mockingly raised her right foot to kick him in the groin. He backed away, laughing, and then a glistening caught the corner of his eye, too. He moved closer to the corpse.

Then he saw it, the golden orb in the corpse’s mouth. Suddenly Sean’s mood changed. He moved slowly, in shock, toward the top of the corpse. Looking at the body upside down, he bent closer to the mouth to see if there was anything else lodged in the throat.

“Was this in her throat all along?” he said, looking up at Maire with an expression that he wore very infrequently. The great Sean Sullivan was in shock. Not an easy thing to do to Sean, shock him, but this clearly was a shock. The second shocked expression in less than ten minutes, a new record!

Maire reached in with her gloved right hand and retrieved the golden orb. Held delicately between thumb and forefinger, the orb gleamed beneath the lights.

“This ball was shoved so far back in her throat, Sean, that at first I could only see a little glint of the gold when I had removed all of that turf from the cavity.”

“Are there any other signs that this might have been murder?” Sean said, as both of them now slipped easily and swiftly into full-on professional mode.

“Not a sacrifice? A murder, you think?” She wanted to know why Sean was so certain about this.

Maire eased the torc away from the neck for a second time, and Sean bent in closer; the indentations from the curvilinear designs on the torc were easily visible to the naked eye.

“Her hands were bound behind her back, Sean,” Maire volunteered freely, knowing that whatever information she gave him he would process quickly with his immeasurable knowledge of Celtic history.

“Still, it could mean it was ritualistic, though I suppose,” he said, drawing a deep sigh inward as if swallowing all the information to digest it and regurgitate it as another hypothesis. Yet he himself was not fully convinced that this was the case.

“The orb was shoved into her throat, and then all this sod was compressed into the oral cavity as well?” he asked, mulling over the information.

Sean moved his eyes from the corpse’s mouth to Maire. She was nodding, a deep, furrowed frown knotting her eye-brows downward, and now she was biting her lower lip.

“I don’t think this one was ritualistic, Maire.” He stood upright and moved toward the sink to begin washing his hands. “Let’s have a look at those discovery site pictures.”

“One more thing,” she said, and she unzipped the body bag entirely away from the bog body. Sean looked astonished. Unable to move or blink, he could only repeat one word.

“Pregnant?” he said, unable to proceed beyond that one word. “Pregnant?”

After a third and final disbelieving “Pregnant?” he knew that this investigation would be one of a life-time. He was thrilled to be part of it and now shared Maire’s gusto for getting the show on the road.

“This is going to be interesting,” he said as he looked at Maire, still nodding and her eye-brows now raised. The golden orb still glistened in her hand as a reminder that it once shone brilliantly to show that this woman was an important person, despite her current condition. The orb that was used to beautify her was also used to kill her.

“She was face-down in the bog, hands tied behind her back, and she was buried upside down.” Maire said, still looking at Sean. This was indeed a revelation in and of itself. Most other victims of ritualistic killings were buried face up, with throats garroted so they would drown in their own blood and hands tied behind their backs, or with their arms pierced with branches to keep them at the bottom of watery bogholes, or decapitated, or disemboweled. This body mimicked those other ritualistic killings in the hands only.

The fact that the woman was pregnant, the torc imbedded into her neck, her mouth stuffed to the bursting point with sod after a golden orb from her hair had been forced down her throat, and her legs visibly lashed or whipped, all of these indicated that this woman had been tortured unlike all other known bog bodies. This was a slow, methodical, and deliberately painful death.

Sean slowly came out of his fog of silent thought and began to talk deliberately and precisely in a staccato-like fashion. The Kerry lilt became softer and sadder.

"This is definitely not a ritual killing, Maire. If she is as old as Old Croghan Man, then a pregnant woman would have been greatly respected. This, I'd bet any money on it, is a murder. They killed her."

"Well done, Mr. Poirot. But who are *they*?"

"What do you want me to do? Solve the whole case in one breath?" He never once looked at Maire. His focus was now entirely on the bog body.

"No, that would be no fun at all."

"I'll wash up, and we'll get started by taking her clothes off," Sean said seriously, without even a hint of humor.

"I have a great one-liner for that!" Maire added as she took the plastic away from the gurney.

"I know, I know!" Sean said, heading toward the sink. "I'll be good at taking her clothes off." He said it without his usual bravado. Focusing on washing his hands and scrubbing up, he looked up and away from the sink to Maire, "I'll have a look at the pictures after we get the dress and ornamentation off and get her in the PEG."

"Sorry, Sean, I was just trying to lighten things up a bit. I suddenly had a mental picture of her last moments on earth, and it wasn't pretty," Maire added.

"Tis all right. But I'll tell you something…" The water filled the room with a sound of newness and energy, and he continued his methodical scrubbing..., "This woman has a hell of a story to tell us. So let's start listening to her." He paused momentarily and then began to dry his hands.

"Her name shall be *Mona*," he said.

"She has a name now?" Maire asked, folding her arms across her chest.

"Of course, remember the Lindow man was dubbed 'Peat Moss' by the British Press?" Sean eyed Maire for some kind of reaction.

"Not really," Maire offered blankly. Then she did a mental flash back to the *News of the World* headline in the eighties. "Oh yeah! Peat Moss! I remember!"

“Well, I swore that if I ever came across a female bog body I would call her Mona,” he said, continuing to dry his hands with vim and vigor and then pulling on the green gloves, snapping them at the wrists. He looked up, not volunteering any more information until she asked for it. He waited.

“Okay, I’ll bite,” said Maire, watching him curiously. “Why *Mona*?”

“Mona,” Sean said, walking back toward the gurney and touching Mona’s hair. “Mona means ‘turf’ right? Like Bord na Mona? The Irish Turf Board?”

“Oh! Right! I like that!” she said, in shocked agreement at such an appropriate name. “Hello, Mona.”

Chapter 5

The Fir Bolgs were an extremist Celtic group that emerged from Belgium to become known as mighty warriors, invading and engulfing other, more placid tribes. Their goal was to expand their territory, having learned from the Romans that land ownership was power.

Expansion was their way of gaining more power, and expand they did. Sometimes young warriors had no choice but to become part of the more extremist group, or else face death. The Fir Bolg were adept at horseback riding, a skill they had developed from their expansion into Turkey. They had abandoned the peaceful existence once known to all Celtic tribes and turned to the slave trade which they had learned in part from their interaction with the Romans.

It was during the Fir Bolgs' expansion as far southward as the Italian Alps and north of the Apennine mountain ranges that the Romans forced them into retreat. The Fir Bolgs were forced to accept that they were no match for the Romans; this was a tremendous blow to their egos.

Driven northward by the Roman Emperor's men, the Fir Bolg Celts had lost the battle for European expansion. They were unrefined in war tactics in comparison to the soldiers of the Roman Empire and were easily defeated. But the Fir Bolgs had learned an important piece of information: people could become assets and therefore be used for trade.

The Romans had indentured servants waiting on their every need or want. Their women wore white tunics and did not fight alongside their men. The Roman women lived to serve their men. It was a lifestyle that greatly appealed to the Fir Bolgs. In their retreat back into mainland Europe, and then to the shoreline of Gaul and Belgium, they manipulated the indentured-servant concept utilized by the Romans and started kidnapping and trading people as slaves.

Women became assets that were owned by men. Men chose their women, with the rule that there was only one man for each woman. It was far easier to keep track of paternity of their children in this way. By making women assets and controlling their sexuality, the Fir Bolgs replaced the mother goddess with their own warrior ethos.

The Fir Bolg faction that emerged from the Belgian Celts had adopted the slave trade whole heartedly by the time they reached Ireland; the kidnapping of people with the sole purpose of doing slave trade with other violent Celtic tribes had become a fine art.

Some slaves were kept as servants, and others as warrior slaves that were used as war fodder. Mostly the slaves were used as trading goods, handed over to other groups, such as the Romans, in exchange for more valuable and exotic items: wine, wine flagons, pelts, blacksmiths, and pine tree resin from the north of Spain, which they used to style their hair into Suebian knots. Lime was used to bleach the hair blonde. The Fir Bolgs looked like no Irish Celts. White hair in tall suebian knots made them stand out among their Irish counterparts.

On the battle field, these white-haired, tattooed warriors seemed to sit tall on their horses; in fact, some were very short and used the Suebian knot to increase their height. They were indeed a very distinct group.

***

All these traits showed that this Fir Bolg tribe had power and influence that reached far beyond Ireland, and therefore the Crannog inhabitants were of little consequence to them.

The people of the crannog sat in crisp midwinter silence as the invaders stood momentarily taking in their new slaves' faces and expressions. Their chieftain was now dead, and the Fir Bolg leader was self-installed as the new chieftain.

The fearsome Fir Bolg warrior pulled Élan even closer to him and snapped his teeth as if he was going to bite her. She pulled backward, and he retained his grip on her arm. She felt his grip tighten, and her arm ached in his hold. He turned to face the natives of the crannog, their faces showing every emotion: disbelief, anger, fear, and astonishment. He had witnessed these faces and emotions many times before.

After many months of discovering and overtaking crannogs and tuatha in Ireland, Colm Riordán knew that this was going to be a relatively easy invasion. His own emotion was one of pride.

Intimidation is the mightiest tool in a warrior's arsenal of weapons. Intimidation of the opponent was done through use of language, tone of voice, eyes, and body movement. So he began the game, using all and every part of his body to emote his fearsomeness. He moved through the gathering of crannog dwellers with the same deliberate moves that the predator uses to trap its prey. Like a hawk circling the skies above, but keeping his eyes on the field mouse below, Colm Riordán's gaze moved from Élan to the crowd.

Still gripping her tightly, he moved through the crowd, using her as an example of his tenacity and strength. No matter how hard she tried to pull away from him, she was no more than a fly in a spider web, struggling for freedom but embroiling itself deeper in captivity. The harder she struggled, the tighter his grasp became.

His voice snarled and carved the air.
“This is our resting site. The more you fight us, the more difficult it will be for you to accept the new order.” He turned his head slowly to eye the spider caught in his web. “As you can see.” Élan tried to pull away from his grasp, but it was impossible to break free.

Despite the difference in accent, the language was similar. He left no doubt to the meaning of his words, for the intonation was gruff and guttural.

“Some of you we will spare. Others we will not. We will decide who lives and dies. This is simple. No?” Here again he turned to face the beautiful young girl struggling to break free from his hold. She refused to look at him. Colm continued on.

“Follow our rules and our ways, and we will spare you. Choose not to do as we say, you will not be spared.”

He tossed Élan aside as if she were a piece of filthy old rags. She stumbled backward and fell against another member of her tribe. This was also a tactic to intimidate the group before him.

Immediately she scanned the crannog for her father's face. When she found it staring at her amidst the crowd and knew he was safe, she felt some relief. He nodded slowly to Élan to indicate that he was unharmed, and he waved his left hand subtly by his side, keeping it low so that only she would see it. Élan recognized the sign immediately from their moonlight hunting times; he was telling her to lie low. Wait for the right time to pounce; this was not the right time. It would come, but this was not the right time.

Liam Ruadh stood close to her father. She saw his face grimace when she fell. He nodded to her softly, agreeing with her father's silent and secret signal to stay where she was. Diarmuid's signal did not go unnoticed by the foreign warrior. Colm Riordán began to move among the natives of the crannog, deliberately moving closer to the faces of the males to see which were warriors and therefore posed potential threats to the invasion and takeover.

"Your way of life has ended. You will now live in the Fir Bolg way." His voice sliced the air throughout the crannog. The warrior strode through the gathered tribal members and watched with amusement as women pulled children closer to them for protection. "Little good that will do." he thought to himself and smiled at them.

In every tuatha, and in every crannog, all behaved the same way. The men who were warriors within the tribe stood with tightened jaws and gritted teeth. Like bubbling volcanoes, they felt the warrior ethos rumble within them. Their expressions gave them away instantly.

Élan's father stood, fists clenched; the muscles of his jaw-line contracted and moved as he tried desperately to control his own fury toward Colm. His nostrils widened and narrowed as he took deep breaths and exhaled through his nose, trying desperately to calm his inner warrior. His eyebrows sloped inward toward the huge knotted furrows on his forehead. His entire demeanor drew the attention of the Fir Bolg leader.

Diarmuid knew this war tactic well; the Fir Bolg circled him slowly and took in his features to determine how much of a threat he posed. The Fir Bolg, Colm, knew by Diarmuid's stance and body language that he was indeed a threat. The body language mirrored that of his own when in battle. It was intimidation in defensive mode. This was what Colm Riordán had been looking for, a potential threat. The crackling frosty footsteps brought Colm Riordán, a Fir Bolg of immense size, to Diarmuid's side.

Colm moved in front of Diarmuid's gaze. It was a stare that looked through Colm, past the crannog and into the forest beyond the fence, not even acknowledging Colm. A strong, deep, blue-eyed gaze into the far-off distance, Diarmuid refused to meet the warrior's gaze eye to eye. Colm eyed his threat from head to toe. After taking in the full picture of the warrior, Colm's scrutiny was caught by the shining silver hanging from Diarmuid's arm.

Colm eyed the wristlet: three intertwined, silver swirls on a strap of leather. He had seen this before, he knew it. Then he looked at Diarmuid's face. It, too, was familiar to him. His mind was whisked backward to the sword in the sunlight, his own blood dripping down its blade onto the cold and wet pebbled beach.

Again he searched for the familiarity in Diarmuid's face. There it was, in the eyes. He saw the same face he looked into when he was but seventeen Imbolcs on the earth. This was the man he had met in battle on the southern coast of Ireland many winters before.

"We know each other, warrior?" The Fir Bolg stood in amazement before Diarmuid, waiting for a response.
Diarmuid shook his head gently to show disagreement. Then he, too, had a vision: the Fir Bolg as a younger man, on both knees and begging to be spared as he held Diarmuid's left arm, clutching it tightly to his chest. Diarmuid then recalled the

voice: “Spare me my life, leave me wounded here, warrior, do not leave me dead!” his blood-stained fingers circled the wristlet.

Diarmuid looked straight into the eyes of Colm Riordán, the Fir Bolg warrior’s stare softened, and so did Diarmuid’s. Colm then reached inside the neckline of his tunic and pulled the triune goddess symbol onto his chest. The Fir Bolg warrior and Diarmuid had indeed met before.
Colm Riordán and Diarmuid stared at each other in disbelief. They saw it reflected in each other’s eyes. Again the mighty Fir Bolg said, “We know each other, warrior?” and he lifted the left sleeve of his tunic to show a large scar that ran diagonally from the elbow to the top knuckle of his thumb. It was a large scar that left nothing to the imagination.

Diarmuid’s mind took him back, and he stood, a young man of twenty-seven years, before a kneeling Belgae Fir Bolg warrior holding his left arm cradled in his right.

The young Belgae Celt had looked upward at the Irish Celt holding his bloody sword aloft. It was the same face that stared back at him today. Diarmuid could easily have killed Colm that day many years ago, but he didn’t. Diarmuid didn’t kill him because the young Fir Bolg Celt, by touching the triune goddess wristlet, the gift from Etain the night that they became man and wife, reminded Diarmuid that he held an even greater power than killing: He held the power to give life. And so the young Fir Bolg was spared.

Here was that same Fir Bolg warrior, with twenty more years on his brow. He stood taller than Diarmuid, his shoulders broader. The Fir Bolg held Diarmuid's left wrist in his hand, and his eyes went from Diarmuid's face to the three silver intertwined swirls on the leather strap.

Diarmuid responded reluctantly, for he was unsure that sparing the young Fir Bolg many years ago would stand in his favor today. The scar on the Fir Bolg's arm was deep and had disfigured it greatly. Diarmuid had marked him. There was no denying their connection.

"We know each other," he said.

Colm placed his hand on Diarmuid's shoulder.

"You granted me life on the southern shores of your land many winters ago. It was you?"

"It was me." Diarmuid took the Fir Bolg's left arm in his right hand and turned it to see the deep disfiguration on the forearm.

"Why did you spare me?" asked Colm, with curiosity. "You could have ended me that day."

"My wife's words came to me as you grabbed my left arm. She told me it was more powerful to give life than to take it. This wristlet was her token of love to me the night we became man and wife. You grabbed this wristlet and asked me to spare you. You wore the same symbol around your own neck. I took it as a sign from the mother goddess that you were to be left alive. I didn't take your life that day; I gave it back to you."

The two opposing warriors spoke quietly to each other. They held each other by the elbows as they continued to speak. The Fir Bolgs and the inhabitants of the crannog watched in disbelief as the two men spoke, holding each other to show their mutual respect and thanks.

Only one person near them could hear their words clearly. Liam Ruadh, the tánaiste, could hear every word. He stood to the left, a little behind Diarmuid. He heard every word of their conversation.

With each word that passed between Colm and Diarmuid, Liam Ruadh could feel their bond strengthen. He knew that the Fir Bolg had gratitude for Diarmuid. He knew that this gratitude would weigh in Diarmuid's favor with the new order of the crannog that the Fir Bolg had proclaimed. He knew that his right to Élan and becoming chieftain were going to be lost in this new order. The moonlight deal reneged upon, and now this new order would put an end to his rights of ownership; over four years of silence to his chieftain about the hunting at night, four years and more of silence and waiting, all for nothing. All would be lost to him in this new regime.

Liam looked at Élan; she sat on the ground waiting like all the others. He saw the fiery look in the Fir Bolg warrior's eyes when he held her close to him. Liam's mind shifted gears quickly, as he began to plot how he could stop all this from happening and secure all the things he had waited for; Élan, submission of women, and the role of chieftain. He saw the dagger hanging by Colm Riordán's side. Then he saw his moment of opportunity, all would not be lost.

The warriors moved to embrace each other. Diarmuid, unsure at first of the intent of Colm's body language, drew backwards. Liam moved to the side and now stood with the two men more directly in front of him. He moved toward both men; Colm indicated with hand gestures and a wholehearted smile to Diarmuid that he wished to give an embrace of gratitude, as Celtic warriors who fought side by side did.

Colm leaned toward Diarmuid; Liam again saw the gleaming dagger dangle by Colm's side. He placed his hand on the handle of the weapon, bending Colm's dagger straight up in its leather strap, the tip pressing on Diarmuid's tunic. The blade, long and with a jagged edge, sliced a deep cut into Diarmuid's left side. Feeling the coldness of the blade tearing his skin, Diarmuid pushed Colm back, and his face became distorted with disbelief, distrust, and anger. Liam Ruadh stepped back and yelled, "Dagger!"

Diarmuid looked at Colm and then at Liam, the blood dripping furiously from his right hand.

"Why?" he asked.

He looked at his wound and watched his own blood gush forth from his abdomen. The coldness of the dagger was more painful than the wound. Diarmuid fell in a bundle on the ground, his face looking up toward Colm Riordán, his eyes moving up Colm's body. No blood stained the fur pelts around Colm's waist or on his clothing. Colm's visage had changed from gratitude to horror.

Diarmuid's body slowly began to fold downward. He turned his head to see Liam rush to his side and push his hands onto the wound. The blood ran forth with the force of an overflowing river. It covered Liam's hands now, stained with blood from stabbing Diarmuid with Colm Riordán's dagger.

Colm saw the blood on Liam's hands. Sensing the Fir Bolg's detection of foul play, Liam fell to Diarmuid's side and pushed his hands into the blood pumping from Diarmuid's body. Diarmuid's blood now covered Liam Ruadh's hands and arms and the front of his body, hiding all traces of his guilty grip on Colm's dagger. The Fir Bolg stood, rooted to the ground with shock, unsure of what had unfolded before him, but he knew that this Celt kneeling beside Diarmuid and tending his wound had attempted to kill his own tribesman.

The Irish Celts broke into riotous uproar and were silenced almost immediately by the rest of the Fir Bolgs. Élan screamed at the top of her lungs. "Father!" She ran to his side and fell to the ground, holding him against her. Liam continued to press his hand onto the wound.

"Do not press him for words, Élan," Liam said as he pressed with great force on the wound. It appeared as if he was trying to stop the bleeding, trying to help. But he pressed with so much pressure that Diarmuid could not speak because of the pain and the loss of breath.

Colm Riordán watched in dismay as both Élan and Liam tried to save Diarmuid. The dagger hung from its leather belt and dribbled blood on the side of his shirt. His hands were unstained. Colm looked at his hands, examined them briefly from all angles, and then looked at Diarmuid. Liam and Diarmuid were drenched in blood. Colm's hands were unstained.

Stunned by the sudden shift in events, Colm Riordán knew that he must continue with the invasion. Unsure of why this had happened, but certain that he had not stabbed Diarmuid, he yelled aloud and gave orders to round up the Irish Celts. Liam Ruadh, the man beside Diarmuid, had stabbed him. Colm knew that this part was true. This red-haired man's hands were stained with blood before he had reached to help Diarmuid. Before Diarmuid fell, he had turned to Liam and asked, "Why?"

Colm, too, wanted to know the answer to this question. Right now he knew that he would continue with the takeover. Diarmuid would die, but Colm Riordán would find out why Diarmuid had been sabotaged by his own tribesman.

"I tell you this day, this man's painful death signals the end to your tribe." Colm's voice boomed above the din of screaming and crying.

"Gather the young men and women and tie them together; leave the children and the elderly," Colm roared to his own men. The other Fir Bolgs immediately sprang into action upon hearing Colm's order to gather and tie the men and women together.

Colm looked downward at Diarmuid and, for the last time, took in the countenance of a man that for years had embodied a hope for all warriors to change their way of life and unite as Celts. Colm looked at Diarmuid, and Diarmuid's gaze became glassy and distant. Élan turned her father's face toward her own. Although he could hear her pleas for someone to save him and for him not to die, Diarmuid slipped into blackness and heard her voice fade off into the dimness as he drifted toward the otherworld.

Then a hand came to his face and twisted it away from Élan's chest, momentarily snapping him away from the edge of unconsciousness.
Diarmuid was a captive of the blue eyes of the Fir Bolg. Liam Ruadh was pushed away, and Colm roared at his men to grab and retain him. Élan remained at her father's side, crying hysterically, losing her breath, listening but confused with their talk.

"I don't understand. Is he one of your men?" Colm whispered, as he held Diarmuid's gaze.

"Yes," came Diarmuid's voice, so weak it was almost incoherent.

"He has blood on his hands. Why would he do this to a tribesman?"

Diarmuid shook his head feebly. "Spare her," he pleaded. Diarmuid's voice was weak, and blood now dripped from his mouth.

"I will find out what happened and why. She will be spared."

He pulled at the leather wristlet, and the band snapped. Colm took it and dangled it in front of Diarmuid's eyes. Diarmuid blinked slowly and nodded his head in agreement. The symbol of the triune goddess of birth, life, and death glittered.

"Take it," Diarmuid said. "Remember the reason I wore it. Keep Élan safe and free."

***

Colm knew that the dagger wound was fatal. Diarmuid was slipping into darkness. Élan knew that she was saying good-bye to her father forever. Her cry became soft. She pulled him closer to her as the Fir Bolg warrior stood upright and tied the leather wristlet onto his left arm. She heard it all but understood nothing. She only knew that her father was now joining her mother in the otherworld.

"Murderer!" she snarled. Diarmuid shook his head and said, "No." Élan believed this to be his fight against death. Colm knew that it was his dagger that had taken Diarmuid's life, but he was now certain that Liam Ruadh's hands had held the dagger.

Why did this Celt sabotage his friend in this way? This question would continue to burn within him.

Élan's cries became a distant echo in Diarmuid's ears as he drifted into darkness and then slumped heavily into her arms. One last shallow breath, and he was gone.

***

"Take her, but do not mark her or harm her," Colm said, removing Diarmuid's body from her arms and laying it on the ground.

"This one will be my servant." He stroked her face and caught her chin in his hand, between his thumb and forefinger, forcing her to look at him. "Your father has asked me to care for you. I gave him my word. You will do as I ask, this is your dying father's wish," he said, with a gentle tone.

Again she felt the hot tears streak down her cheeks and burn her eyes.

"Your 'word' is the word of a villainous murderer! It means nothing to me or my father." Her anger was so vibrant and alive that Colm knew she would not believe him if he tried to explain what had happened. He would do so later, when the reality of her situation sank in and she had calmed.

"Take her with the others, but treat her gently," Colm said to the other Fir Bolg, who smiled a sordid smile.

"Your prize?"

"Yes," he said, and handed her over. If this was how he had to protect her, then he'd allow it.

"This isn't happening. This isn't real. How could our home have been destroyed in an instant?" thought Élan, as she was led to a group of twenty-three of the healthiest men and women of the tribe.

Her mind raced backward to her morning activities in the forest and how abruptly all harmony had come to an end. Her body began to convulse into shock. She began to breathe irregularly, trying desperately to catch her breath and breathe deeply. Her entire body was shaking and shivering; she felt her breath stop, and her head thumped onto the Fir Bolg warrior's chest. The warrior held her upright by the shoulders momentarily; she had lost consciousness, but she convulsed. It was all too much for her to comprehend or take in. Colm watched her convulse and took five huge steps across the crannog floor to grab her. He hoisted her over his shoulder. She draped lifelessly across his body.

When she came to from her state of darkness, she smiled briefly with relief: Had she dreamt it all? Then she realized it was not a dream, that her losses were real and painful. She was aware that she was propped against the Fir Bolg's body and riding on his horse, and the smells and accents snapped her back into harsh reality: all that was familiar was now lost. She saw the crannog disappear behind them into the distance, hidden by the once familiar forest.

"Please don't take me from my home," she pleaded, and Colm was suddenly aware that she was conscious again.

"You have a new home now," he responded, "With me."

In truth, Colm Riordán was also in shock at the events of the morning. He wanted nothing more than to believe that the warrior on the southern shores of Ireland many years earlier had deliberately spared him his life and that this was his day to bestow his thanks and gratitude on this warrior. His mind was far from Élan, whose head rested against the nape of his neck. His stare was into the distant evergreens before him, and his mind blackened.

As the sunlight streaked in shafts of light through the trees, Colm pondered why a warrior would be killed by one of his own tribesmen. This question gnawed at him. No Fir Bolg would have behaved like this toward another.

Élan spotted Liam traipsing through the forest ahead of her. Tied together with at least twenty other tribal men and women, Liam Ruadh had been spared, for now. He walked with his head bent low and stumbled now and again over rocks and tree roots. Unsteady steps through the slimy, mossy forest floor and slippery, frosty rocks made the group move at a slow pace.

Liam looked disillusioned, staring blankly at the forest floor. The front of his tunic and his hands were covered in blood. His hands were covered in red wetness.

Élan tried to lift her head away from Colm's chest and was warned not to with a soft, "Stay easy." It was then she noticed that her hands and feet were bound with roping. Élan smelt scented oil on his clothing. He smelled of salt and freshness.

"Where are we going?" she asked.

"Have you ever seen the sea of Ireland?"

"No," came her reply. Though she had never been to the Irish Sea she knew that it was far away from the shores of Lough Derg. Therefore, he was taking her far away from her home, and she became filled with grief and sadness again. She had lost her home and her father, all within moments. She tried to hold it back, but the tears came again, and the warrior felt the hot wet drips falling on his forearms as he held the horse's reins.

"Dromanagh," he said, trying to prevent another tantrum from erupting. "Your little island is very beautiful, and you have only seen Lough Derg and your own crannog. Dromanagh overlooks the Irish Sea. It is a very beautiful sight." Colm's eyes fixated on Liam Ruadh, ahead in the distance.

"Why? How far away is it?" Élan asked again, fearful that the answer would confirm her deepest fears. So far that she would never see her own crannog again?

"Two day's ride on horseback, it is not far at all," he replied, and then added, "My resting place there is beautiful. It sits a-top of a hill, and the scenery around it compares to no other."

She looked ahead again for Liam's figure and felt at ease when she saw him still ahead, traipsing suspiciously through the forest. Despite the fact that Liam and her father were not close, it was comforting to Élan that the man who had tried to save Diarmuid was part of the group being taken to Dromanagh Fort.

"Why am I being carried on horseback while the others are walking?" she asked, for it had suddenly dawned on her that there were women her age and older walking too.

"You fainted, and I carried you until you were well enough to walk," Colm responded, trying to put her at ease. She sensed the softness in his voice and instinctively knew that it was an attempt to win her over.

"I am well enough to walk now," was her abrupt response to his gentle explanation.

"Good," he said heartily, letting her slide from his grasp down the side of the horse until her feet touched the forest floor. He was not in any mood to try to win her favor. Another Fir Bolg, riding alongside Colm, dismounted upon orders and cut the ropes at her feet. When she was standing on the ground, she called out to Liam.

Upon hearing his name, Liam turned around. He was covered in blood, his hands and the front of his torso stained red. The name did not go unnoticed by Colm. Had he killed Diarmuid by mistake? Did this Liam want Diarmuid dead because of a tribal dispute? Why would this young girl befriend the possible murderer of her own father? This was a strange end to an even stranger day.

“Let it play out by itself,” he thought. “This Liam needed Diarmuid dead for a reason. Was she the reason?”

The captives trudged steadily through the forest. When they came into a clearing, the sun had moved from the mossy side of the trees to the opposite side, and it was lower in the sky. They had walked a long time and were glad to see a dwelling appear before them. They were tied together again in a large meeting house. The land was flat here, and green and grassy. Even in winter this area of Ireland seemed shaded from the harsher winter winds that swept through the crannogs of the coastline and along the rivers. It was for this reason that the Fir Bolgs used it as their first halting site on their route to do slave trade with the Roman settlement on the coastline of Dublin.

Slaves were traded for wine and produce from mainland and southern Europe, and for fine goods such as horses, oils, jewelry, coins, and exotic foods and clothes. The Romans did not use their new people as objects to trade. They handed slaves over to renowned families to become indentured servants. In turn, the Romans were granted great favors to travel and conquer and explore the lands and waters. This group of Irish Celts would be handed over to the Romans living at the coastal settlement of Dromanagh, and later traded for expansion favors in Europe.

As his men tied the new slaves together, after they had received a meal of meat and water, Colm moved Diarmuid's wristlet between the fingers of his right hand. They would reach the coastal settlement in three more days of walking. He would trade all of this new group, all but one, but first he would know the reason why Diarmuid's murderer was close to his daughter. He would come to know the truth behind Diarmuid's death.

He looked at the wristlet on his left arm and traced the swirls with his forefinger. He watched with great interest as Élan sat beside Liam. Had they both planned to eliminate Diarmuid? Was this a joint act? Was she innocent in all of this, or did she stand to gain something from her own father's death? Only time would tell.

"Better to be rid of disloyal and untrustworthy Celts. The Irish are indeed wild," he mused to himself, and continued to observe the interaction between Liam and Élan.

Colm wanted to devise a plan to get Liam Ruadh to confess. That plan would take shape at Dromanagh, the Roman settlement at Loughshinny on the eastern coast of Ireland, the Fir Bolg's final halting site and trading post with the Romans.

Colm continued to swirl the wristlet on his arm absentmindedly. He looked up and smiled sarcastically across at Liam and Élan.

Liam Ruadh looked away. Élan returned his stare and then bent her head over her knees.

'Birth, life and death," Colm whispered to himself, as his fingers traced the interlocking swirls on the wristlet. He had promised to spare her; she seemed genuinely distraught that her father had been killed. His greatest job would be to convince her that Liam had killed Diarmuid. Tonight the Fir Bolg warriors would each take turns on watch. Tomorrow they would press on toward the eastern shore of Ireland.

Chapter 6

It had been five weeks since Mona had made the journey from Boteen's bog in North Tipperary to the National Museum in Dublin. Her clothes had been removed, dusted off, cleaned by a nonabrasive method, and put on a standard museum mannequin in an air tight glass chamber on display in the "Celtic Hordes" section of the museum. The chamber was then flooded with inert argon gas to prevent any further deterioration of the clothing.

It was like no other piece of Celtic clothing ever found, in any country in Europe. The richness of the deep red dress and the golden trims on the sleeves and hemline were possibly the finest displays, in all of Europe, of the intricate art work performed by Celtic blacksmiths. Many photographs had been taken and emailed to various Celtic art historians throughout Europe. One professor from the Celtic department of the University of Wales declared:

The intricacies of the curvilinear vines and leaves and the animals bodies are reminiscent of the La Tène period.

However the larger square centerpiece of the waistline is most definitely displaying a Roman influence. It is rather unusual to have the two together.

After much thought about doing forensic testing on the clothing to determine its age, a consensus was reached between Maire and Sean. Mona herself was in such a remarkably good state of preservation that they would use her only to determine the age of the body and the season of death. The clothing would remain undamaged by testing. And so it was put on display for the world to see.

The state pathologist was making her second attempt to come and study the body today in order to determine the cause of death. Since Maire and Sean had both stripped Mona, they had seen all the wounds and lashes, but only Sarah Bohane, the state pathologist, would be able to legally determine and record the cause of death.

Bohane's first attempt at making her way to the museum's forensics lab was a disastrous effort due to a massive bus strike. Trying to get from her office across the city to the museum was like getting a rocket to Pluto—, impossible.

Every Taxi had been grabbed by tourists it seemed. The streets were giant car parks, and traffic had congested so heavily people took to the streets in such volume that they shuffled, not walked, on the footpaths.

"I think I'll have to postpone the visit until next week or so," she informed Maire over the phone. "Isn't this the second CIE strike in a year?"

"No. I think the last one was in the summer last year. Wasn't it?"

"Well, unfortunately, by the time I would get there it would be so late we'd be packing up and going home. I will have a look at my calendar and see what's available."

The next available date was four weeks later. Mona had floated aimlessly face-down in polyethylene glycol solution whilst Sarah Bohane, and her husband and son traveled to Tuscany, Rome, Venice, and various other parts of Italy for their summer holidays. Two weeks of relaxation for Bohane, then two weeks of catch-up at work, and today was the moment she would meet the well-preserved Mona.

The PEG solution kept the tissue soft. The body was in such a supple state of preservation that Maire and Sean both felt somber when they saw Mona out of the PEG and on the examiner's table. It was indeed the full body of a pregnant woman.

Maire felt a great urgency to treat this body with respect and a great need to discover as much as forensic testing could possibly tell her about Mona's life. Mona was a corpse, not a bog body. Mona was not a fragmented, dismembered, dried-up carcass. She was a tanned, supple, whipped, pierced, and tortured pregnant corpse.

Gallagh Man, Meenybradden Woman, and the other bog bodies at the museum were shrunken, dried-out shells of beings. Mona, although she didn't look fairly recently deceased, almost had a personality. As Maire, Sean, and two other forensic archaeologists assigned to the investigation lifted Mona's body out of the PEG solution, they let her drip dry over the tub and then moved her to the table. Naked as the day she was born, nothing left to hide.

"I hope she's not going to be late, or we'll have to put her back in the drink," said Sean, pulling his top lip down with his lower lip and shaking his head.

"You look a bit annoyed Sean," said Maire as she gently moved Mona's hair back from her face.

"Sure, any ejit could tell you how she died. I mean, ya just have to look at the wounds in her ankles, and the lashes on her lower legs. Mrs. Hot Shit has to take four weeks to get here, and we can't do any testing on the body in case we tamper with evidence?"
"It's the law; you can't do anything about it." Maire was upset over the four-week wait too but she knew that there was nothing that could be done about it.

Their musings were interrupted with an abrupt, "She's here," from one of the other archaeologists, who was standing at the window and eyeing the parking lot for Bohane's BMW. Bright blue, you couldn't miss it, or the speed at which she drove it.

"Did you leave her a space near the door?" Maire asked Sean, who made a point of parking next to the handicapped parking space, the closest parking space to the lab entrance door, every day. The shortest distance to walk from car to lab and lab to car was Sean's idea of car park dictatorship. That was his spot!

"Sure and begorra, I did," he said, and he smiled smugly, folding his arms across his chest in defiance.

When Sarah Bohane looked at the space she had parked in, instead of seeing a sign that read "Reserved" at the front of her car, she read, "Head Bottle Washer," in black marker on lined

A4 paper. She shook her head and exited the car, rounded the front of the BMW, lifted the A4 sheet, crumpled it up into a tight ball, and made her way to the examination room.

"Oh, shit!" a voice exclaimed from the window.
"What?" said Sean, acting very innocently as he started to prepare the implements required for the examination.

"She's bringing the sign in," came the reply.

"What sign?" said Maire, looking from the window to Sean. He laughed and tilted his head sideways, lifting his hand to his ear as if listening acutely for something, some sound off in the distance..

There they were; the footsteps, sharp, smart, and clipping in the hallway. Clip, clip, clip, clip.

"Them shoes are all about business!" he laughed, and then the door opened and a crumpled-up piece of paper hit him between the eyes.

"Stop messing with me, Sullivan, or I'll file for harassment." holding a large black hand-bag over her right arm, a bronzed and well-dressed Sarah Bohane, state pathologist, had arrived.

"Well, hello Mrs. Bohane. It's good to see you again," said Sean, in a tone of over-done respect.

Bohane had worked with Sean before, on a few different cases, and his humor just didn't work with her. She did not appreciate his disrespect for her higher position, but she did like the attention. It was a strange juxtaposition of emotions for her. She did what she always did when she was placed in situations she couldn't control or felt uncomfortable in; she used sarcasm. It only made matters worse.

Sean sensed how uncomfortable she was in his presence, and he went for the jugular. Sarah Bohane was no different than anyone else in the room, in Sean's eyes, so he would take her off her high horse with a quip or two to bring her back to earth.

"How are you, Maire?" Bohane asked.
"Great. Thanks!"

"So this is the big day," said Bohane, leaving her bag on the counter and unbuttoning her sleeves and then rolling them up.

"Yes, very excited to hear what your conclusions are as to the cause of death," said Maire, standing protectively next to Mona.

"Yes," came the Kerry lilt. "We think she died in a horrific traffic accident actually. You might be able to help us sort it out."

"Oh! Did they have cars back in Celtic times, Sean," said Sarah as she scrubbed up and then dried robustly, her back to Sean all the time.
"Oh, God, no! She was on her way to a turf sale and got trampled by a herd of mammoth in the bog!"

There were a few stifled giggles among some staff members.

"Don't encourage him," said Bohane, pulling on the latex gloves and making her way, in an almost disinterested fashion, toward the table.

"He brings out the worst in people," Bohane continued, and then she looked at Sean. "Traffic accident, definitely." She did have a sense of humor, sometimes. Now the other museum staff members laughed, because it was her joke, and they felt safe.

"Well, those holes in the ankles are not typical, are they?" Bohane's hands gently touched Mona's legs.

"No," said Sean, as he walked to the table. The two holes were about one inch above the ankles. Bits of woven sally rod remained in the holes. He had slipped into his professional mode.

“Would a bit of this sally rod help with a carbon-14 dating?” she asked, as she brought the tweezers in her right hand up from the wound and dropped a small fragment of the sally rod into a petri dish.

“We were going to do metal composition testing on some of the decoration and ornamentation on the clothing, but decided against it,” offered Maire.

“Oh, yes. I must have a look at the clothing on my way out. I hear it is very impressive indeed,” Bohane answered.

By the time Sarah Bohane had finished scrutinizing, prodding, and poking Mona, the cause of death was clear as crystal.

“Let me demonstrate on you, Maire, if I may?” Bohane began her evaluation.

Using Maire as her model, Sarah showed them that the various wounds and markings on Mona’s body led her to believe that Mona was tortured and buried alive upside down.

The sally rod remnants in the wounds in her ankles and the distortion of the skin around the wounds led Bohane to believe that Mona was suspended upside down.

"Now, whether this was done over a boghole or from a tree I can't tell you. But if you look carefully at the direction the skin has been pulled in by the sally rod, she was definitely hanging upside by her ankles."

Bohane continued on, methodically, up the limbs of the body. "The lashes across the legs are self-explanatory. Pure and simple, I think she was being tortured to death, but it was slowly done so it would last longer."

Bohane then brought Maire's hands behind her back. "This was done so she couldn't fight back, obviously."

She then walked to the front and placed her hands around Maire's neck. The Torc marks were significant to her theory that Mona was hanging upside down during all of this.

"Now I haven't seen the torc itself yet, but Sean, you'd be able to help me here."

"Fire ahead," Sean retorted.

“Well, aren’t Celtic torcs supposed to rest casually on the nape of the neck and a-top of the collar-bone?”

“Yes, definitely! Right here, like this,” showing her the area where the torc would have rested on his neck.

“Well, that answers two questions for me, then!” Bohane walked from Maire and back to Mona, pointing to the torc markings on her neck.
“Do you see how high up the strangulation marks are on the neck?” They all bent in to get a closer look at the markings.

“Well, she would have had to be hanging upside down for the torc to be up so high on her neck. Which means the attacker would have had to be standing on solid ground. Whoever did it, though, didn’t want her to die that way. They didn’t want to strangle her to death.”

“How can you tell that?” asked Maire.

“The airways are still open at the torc marks. She smothered to death from the golden torc and all the peat that was rammed into her mouth.” She shook her head slowly as she eyed Maire and Sean.

“This is some bog body you have here,” Bohane said.

The group gathered nodded in agreement.

“Have you done the high-resolution CAT scan yet?” Bohane inquired, touching a green, latex covered hand over the pregnant belly.

“We are all lined up for the lab at two today.”

“I am dying to see what the 3-D computer imaging will show us,” said Maire. “I know she is extremely well preserved, but I’ll bet anything that the 3-D computer images will show her to be a beauty altogether,” she said, looking at Mona’s face and envisioning her own image of a beautiful Celtic woman.

“It was probably her beauty that was the cause of it,” said Bohane again, shaking her head. “It should be interesting, though. I’d love to be kept informed of your findings, if I may.”

“Is that the official cause of death then, being too gorgeous?” said Sean with a crooked smile that made the rest of the group snap back into the present.

Sensing that he had over-stepped the mark with this last comment to Bohane, Sean immediately attempted to back pedal with professional gusto.

"I know this is going to be a tremendously sad case folks, but standing around shaking our heads sorrowfully at her won't do any good either," he said, raising his eyebrows and widening his eyes.

"I hate to admit it, but he is right, and I have to run," said Bohane, looking at the wall clock, then taking the gloves off and tossing them in the rubbish bin.

"Cause of death would be choking, Sean. Not strangulation with the torc, but being forced to swallow the golden orb and the peat. In fact, she may have still been alive and aware when they lowered her into the boghole. They may have just stuffed her mouth to stop her from screaming. I'd rather live in the north side of Dublin and take my chances than live in Celtic times, I tell you!"

"Don't forget to look at the clothing that she was wearing," Maire reminded Bohane as she retrieved her bag.

"Do I have the time?" Bohane said, glancing at the wall clock again.

"I have ten minutes. Right! I will be talking to you. Let me know what you come up with as a result of further testing?"

"Indeed we will," said Sean, holding the door open for her.

"You behave yourself." She grinned at him good-naturedly and winked at Maire as she departed. "Bye, now."

"Thanks very much," he called after her, as she clipped her way back down the hall and headed to the main public section of the museum.
"I would never have picked up on the angle of the torc on her neck," he said, walking back to Mona and looking at her neck. "I suppose state pathologists are useful after all!"

"I wonder what she did to deserve all of this?" Maire wondered aloud as she prepared Mona for her dip back into the PEG solution.

"Sure, we may never find that out, my dear," replied Sean, and she knew that could be very true.

The four museum workers prepared Mona for her next trip. The CAT scan would reveal the internal organs and help create the 3-D computer image which would eventually become the model of Mona. Maire wondered if the baby would be visible on the scan, too. They had little time to waste, as Mona had to be returned to the PEG solution within the next two hours.

The body was covered over like any corpse would be and wheeled to the exit doors. The ambulance had been waiting for about ten minutes, but the driver knew that he was picking up the mysterious bog body found in Tipperary weeks earlier, so he didn't complain about the wait. There was no rush as far as he was concerned, and he was getting paid by the hour.

The stretcher bumped through the doors and rolled out into the summer morning. It was a cool day, but promised to rain by late afternoon. The lab with scan availability for that time that was nearest to the Museum was in the Rotunda Hospital, so they headed toward the busiest part of the city and tried to beat lunch-hour traffic.

Sean and Maire sat in the back of the ambulance with Mona; both had become protective of her over the course of the last four weeks or so. They were both anxious to see what the scan would reveal internally. Now that the State pathologist was completing her report, they were free to continue with further forensic testing.

Other than the occasional glance at each other and then at Mona, the ambulance ride was uneventful. They had managed to snake their way fairly easily from Nassau Street up along to College Street and then made a straight run across the river Liffey on D'Olier Street toward the Rotunda hospital.

Hospitals, for Sean, were the reason he never went into regular medicine. He acted strangely in hospitals, and you could sense his unease; he didn't even try to hide how uncomfortable he was. As the Rotunda came into view, he shifted uneasily in the back of the ambulance and said, "Well, here we go," with about as much vigor as a deflating balloon.

"You'd have made a great Doctor," said Maire mockingly. "What's the matter with you? You're as uneasy as a bag of cats right now."

"I could never stand hospitals. I spent Christmas in hospital in Tralee when I was eleven. A full two weeks because of complications from getting my tonsils out. I hated every minute of it." This was a rare sighting, a scared Sean Sullivan.

"Did they not take good care of you?" Maire inquired as she prepared to unload Mona.

"No, they were grand. It was all the people walking around sick and bawling their eyes out. Hospitals are very unhappy places."

"True enough. Brave it out, though, we'll be here for about an hour or so, and we should be back at the museum by four o'clock at the latest." There it was, the short glimpse of the vulnerable side to Sean Sullivan: rare but not nonexistent. It was these rare glimpses of vulnerabilities that made her like him. He was a child-like man.

For all the bravado and joking around, he was just an insecure, frightened little boy at heart. He responded to her excited face with a very false, beaming "happy" smile, and they both laughed. The brakes screeched as the ambulance drew to a stop.

"We're here!" Maire said, heading toward the back doors of the ambulance.

The afternoon sunlight flooded into the back of the ambulance and blinded them both for a moment. Within minutes, Mona was in the computed tomography scanner of the Rotunda hospital's ground-floor Unit 3-B.

Mona was placed on the bed of the CAT scanner, and then she disappeared into the tunnel of the machine, like any other patient. The technician brought the images up on the computer, announcing each body part as the gray, black, and white images scrolled onto the screen systematically.

The head had no wounds whatsoever. It was untouched. The skull was intact and had no breaks, holes, or cracks that showed trauma. The upper torso, from the shoulders down to the waist, showed breakages to some of the ribs, and the pregnant belly revealed the small, almost undetectable skeleton of a fetus in the seventh or eighth month of development. It was about eighteen inches long, according to the technician's estimation from the gray image on the screen.

"Now, in the Laci Petersen case in America in 2003, the child was expelled from the body in coffin birth? Why didn't that happen here?" Sean mused aloud, as he narrowed his eyes to try and sharpen his image of the picture on the computer screen.

"She was upside down, Sean," Maire said in a mono-toned voice.
"Gravity was in play, the fetus remained inside because of the force of gravity, I'd say." She looked at the technician, and he nodded at her.

"More than likely it was the fact that she was upside down and the peat was thrown in a-top of her. This is a remarkable bog body find. When you do the 3-D imaging, the results should be fantastic."

"We are taking her back to do the carbon-14 testing today." Maire was anxious to see what the CT scan would reveal about the sally rod roping shoved through her knees and ankles.

"Can we look at the legs and see what was done there? We found remnants of sally rod roping in the wounds."

The technician pressed more buttons, and the computer screen slowly filled with the gray, black, and white imaging of the thigh and knee areas. The rods had been pushed through the knees, and further down the same was true of the ankles.

"She was staked into the bog, and then buried upside down?" The technician looked at Sean when he spoke. "Not possible," he said, removing his glasses and rubbing his eyes.

"Why wouldn't that be possible?" said Sean.
"The boghole would have been filled with water. How would anyone have been able to actually stand and do this in a boghole? It would be like standing in quick-sand. The killer would have sunk with her. That scenario is impossible."

"He's right." Maire nodded, and then something struck her. "How strong is sally rod when it is braided like a rope?"

"It won't break too easily," said the technician.
"How do you know that?" said Maire, smiling from Sean to the technician, amazed that he had such a wealth of information about the sally rod.

"A sally rod," he said, swiveling in his computer chair, and facing them with authority, "is a willow branch that is braided. We used it to drive the cattle from field to field when we needed to let them graze new grass. Then my father used it on us to drive us harder in school, but that was the seventies for you!" He laughed as he swiveled back to the computer screen.

"Where are you from?" Maire inquired.

"Nenagh, Tipperary North Riding," he replied in a fake, posh, English accent.

"The bog where the body was discovered was about twelve to fifteen miles away from Nenagh, on the County Galway border. Do you know the area?" asked Maire.

"If it was near the Portumna area, I would know it. Carrigahorrig and Terryglass?" he asked to see if the place names were significant.

"The closest town was Portumna, but the bog was on the Tipperary side of the Shannon. Booteen's bog?"

"Never heard of it," he replied. "I do know that there are boglands in that area, but I wouldn't know the names or owners or anything like that."

"The border issue is important, though, I think," Sean interrupted casually. "I think that might be something we might want to learn more about later on."

"Well, you found her on the border of Galway and Tipperary, that's all I can tell you," the CAT scan technician said.

The sally rod, it was discussed and generally agreed upon, had been roped in one long piece through both knees, and also through the ankles. All were in agreement that the pulling of the sally rod though the flesh must have hurt like hell. The lashes on the calves showed up like black stripes on the screen. Mona was tortured but not enough to kill her.

As the technician scrolled the images back up the legs, abdomen, and torso, a strange shadow in the region of the esophagus caught their eyes. It was circular but flat. When the technician zoomed in on the image, he suddenly realized that there were at least four or five more of these disks at the opening to the stomach and in the stomach.

"What are they?" said Maire, leaning closer to the screen.

"That's the best imaging I can give you. You might have to get invasive if you want any more details on the contents of the stomach."

Simultaneously, Sean and Maire chimed, "Endoscope."

"The tissue might rupture, so I'd be very careful. If you were to do an examination on her stomach to see its contents, you'd have to do surgery, right?" said the technician.

"No, forensic testing of the fingernails and hair follicles can tell us that information without doing open surgery."

"Ultra-sound?" Maire said, waiting for approval or applause, whichever came first. Sean pulled his mouth sideways, his eyebrows went upward in thought, and then he said, "Might work…, sure, it's worth a shot."

"We'll try the ultra-sound before the endoscopy." Maire again leaned closer to the screen to see if the imaging gave any further clues as to what these disks actually were; right now, they were nothing but hazy grayness.

"I have burned the entire procedure on a disk as we were working, so you can take it with you and examine it further. That's all I can do for you here on my end," said the technician, bending over to retrieve the disc from the computer tower. He wrote on the cover: "CAT Scan Bog Body North Tipperary August 17th 2004."

"What time is it?" said Maire, distractedly looking beneath her sleeve for her watch. It was almost three fifteen.

"Oh God, we'd better get moving or we'll be sitting in rush hour traffic until dawn."

The bog body was lifted gently back onto the stretcher and a white sheet draped over her. The negotiation amongst traffic was a little more difficult at this time. The journey along D'Olier Street and Nassau Street was slower, as tourists drove haphazardly trying to find their way to Trinity and the Book of Kells. At last, Maire saw the "Kildare Street" sign on the corner of the red brick building.
"Straight into the PEG with her, yeah?" She looked at Sean for approval.

"We'll use that splinter of that sally rod Sarah Bohane took from her ankle earlier and get started on the carbon-14 dating of it." Maire added hastily.

"I am dying to know her age," Sean said, as they emerged from the back of the ambulance and rattled Mona back inside the

Museum lab. Mona was returned gingerly into the PEG solution. She'd had a hectic day.

Chapter 7

The weary band of Irish Celts traipsed in a stumbling, listless line up the hill to the Roman settlement. Four days had now passed since the Fir Bolg invasion of the crannog.

As they made their way through a wooden gateway, it suddenly became apparent that they had entered the crannog of a very large and prosperous tribe.

Their feet no longer trudged through grass and heather; each step they took now made a sound on the stone roadway beneath them. This was a foreign sound to them. Even the horses seemed to sense the difference, as they became slightly unsteady and their riders pulled a little tighter on the reins. Their hooves pulled to grip the smooth stone surface, and the sound brought attention to the visitors.

People began to appear from the stone dwellings mottled all around the Roman settlement. The Romans were superior in architecture and infrastructure, but the Celtic Fir Bolgs were by far the superior horsemen.

This crannog did not have a wooden fence around it; it had a stone wall that stood about three men high. The wall was wide enough for men to walk a-top of it easily, without fear of falling due to a misstep.

The view from the top of this hill was breathtaking. Below them lay the serene and sandy shores of Loughshinny. Low ledges of rock gave way to a flat, slowly sloping beach about a quarter of a mile square, making it possibly the best harbor on the entire eastern coastline of Ireland. Most other harbors on the coastline of Ireland held the promise of certain scuttling of ships as their bows scraped themselves into shreds on the jutting, jagged, rocky shores. Loughshinny was flat, a safe haven for boats.

The Dromanagh hilltop fort was sheltered, secluded, and safe. Only the occasional breeze from the west was felt; otherwise it was a sheltered and still settlement for the Romans.

The Romans had come to, seen, and conquered a very scenic and valuable piece of Irish land, and they secured their strong hold on Irish soil by making this a Roman fort abroad. The harbor was theirs, too. Over five thousand Roman people lived here at Dromanagh Fort.

Élan had never seen the coastline before. Her fatigue and astonishment at the view toward the base of the hill were overwhelming. She tripped and fell to her knees, and despite her awareness of how bad her situation was, she couldn't help but stare off into the distance and see with wonder the things she had only heard her father describe in the tales he told of his travels.

The waves struck the rocks with force, then thundered a distinctive "whoosh" and sprayed a white veil of droplets into the air and onto the beach. White birds swirled in the sky above. The air smelled vibrant and alive; it even tasted different.

To her left stood stone structures; like the case in her own crannog; children played outside and mothers called their names. The structures were bigger and built in straight shapes, with no curves, unlike the huts of straw and branches and mud on the crannog. Straight black boxes stood out among the gray stones, revealing darkness inside these structures. Occasionally Élan saw a white-draped body move through the darkness and realized that these openings were like the doors of the huts, but higher up.

The children hopped through the gardens that separated the stone houses from the roadway. Élan could see their robes clearly amongst the tall maize that stood crispy and dry and beheaded of its nourishment. All the children wore white garments, and their skin seemed to be the color of bulrushes on the river Shannon, a light golden brown.

As the captives were driven along the stone roadway, children danced up to greet them. Their language was different. Their eyes, darker than their skin, were as black as the night sky. Élan's pale skin and green eyes were an oddity to these children.

"Ecco l'occhi!" they chanted, for they had rarely seen such green in human eyes before. Their mothers yelled, "Andiamo!" from the distance, but the children tugged and hopped alongside these seemingly odd humans.

To the left of the roadway stood larger stone structures; it was hard to tell from the roadway if they were also dwellings or meeting houses. Some had large pillars to either side of the entrance ways. White limestone was used for these pillars and gave the buildings the appearance of having two large, white teeth. "Not an inviting look for a dwelling," thought Élan.

One of the Fir Bolg warriors galloped ahead and motioned for the captives to follow him onto another roadway. This one moved away from the frost-dried maize grasses and verged to the left. It led straight past another low, stone-wall fence into the larger stone buildings.

The road divided and circled and split among all the large stone structures. Their road led them into a rectangular courtyard, bordered on all sides by tall stone houses. The only way out was the way they came in.

On either side of the stone entrance way was a man wearing a red knee length tunic, over which he wore a leather smock adorned with golden embellishments along the edges. The men's heads were covered with golden-colored hats with red bristles down the middle, from front to back. Over their shoulders they had strapped large pelts of brown fur that covered them from shoulder to ground. Their feet had leather straps bound around the foot, all the way up to their knees. Each man held a weapon like the sword used by the Fir Bolg to kill the chieftain, but these weapons were shorter than the sword.

They motioned with their weapons that the captive Celts were to move to the center of the courtyard. As the Fir Bolgs and their horses made their way into the courtyard, behind the Celts, the two men either side of the entrance pulled a rope, and large wooden gates swung from either side of the entrance-way and met in the middle to create a perfectly measured obstruction to freedom. The two men stood back in their original positions and held a straight standing pose. The Celtic men and women stared, incredulous that these two men now obstructed their way back to freedom.

“Welcome to Dromanagh Fort!” came a heavily accented male voice from behind the group. As the Fir Bolg warriors dismounted their horses the Celts turned to see the man that would be their “owner.”

Unlike the slave trade used by the Fir Bolgs, the Romans would use these Celts as indentured servants. The Celts would show the Roman settlers how best to use the land, which animals to hunt and eat, and the fish that were safe to eat, and in return for cleaning, and cooking for and serving the Romans, they would be offered protection and a dwelling place within the walls of Dromanagh fort.

Their new “owner” was dressed in similar fashion to the men standing guard on either side of the entranceway. He had no hair on his face, and his mop of black hair was left unadorned by the strange-looking hat worn by the others. His eyes too were as black as a dark night. The leader of the Fir Bolgs greeted the dark-skinned man, and they then embraced. There was some gruff laughter between them, and the Fir Bolg, Colm Riordán, turned to face his group of slaves.

.

“I will keep a few for myself, Antonio, but only four or so. The rest are yours. All I ask is that you let me choose my own four and give us a place to sleep for a few nights. We will make our way back to Belgae at the first sign of a calm sea."

"Your ships are ready. It has been a mild fortnight since your departure from us. How fared you in the wilds of Ireland?" asked the Roman, in the very broken and slowly spoken Celtic tongue that the Fir Bolgs used as their native language. Years of trade and business dealings with the Fir Bolgs had made many Romans realize that it was important to learn some of this awkward language; expansion and survival depended on it.

"This country is tree heavy and land light. I thought my own country had trees…," here Colm laughed and then continued on. "To the west and south are treacherous, useless lands. I lost two men and their horses in rivers with no bottoms. They were swallowed into the earth. The rest of the time we maneuvered between trees in heavy, dark forests. Not worth anything except for its people."

"The Empire spreads throughout Britannia. Some battles emerge but remain futile against Roman soldiers and armies."

"When will the Roman Empire end its expansion?' asked the Fir Bolg, wondering if, should the Romans choose to end their trade dealings with the Fir Bolgs, they too be would assimilated into the Roman empire.

"Only the Emperor can answer that; he commands, and we obey. That is why I am here in Ireland instead of prosperous, sunny Rome."

The sun did not shine too often or for too long in Ireland. The Roman Emperor had commanded the settlement at Loughshinny for two reasons. The first was to determine if Ireland had natural resources that would be valuable to Rome and therefore make it worthwhile to invade. The second, if Ireland had no valuable natural resources, was that it could serve the purpose of becoming a prison colony for the Roman empire. This could rid the empire of thieves, murderers, and traitors by shipping them off to a small remote island in the west of Europe, with no way off.

The Roman settlement had been at Loughshinny for only twenty moon cycles now, and the Fir Bolgs' knowledge of the country and its terrain came in useful to the Romans.

"How many in total?" asked the Roman, wandering through the ragged band of Irish Celts.

"We have twenty-three."

"And this beauty?" said the Roman, as he halted directly in front of Élan and immediately felt the intensity of emotion penetrating from her green-eyed gaze at him. Her bottom jaw was clenched so tightly that her facial muscles went into a convulsive spasm.

Liam Ruadh surged with anger. She was his! He pushed forward, his broad shoulders parting the two Celts before him. His blue eyes were rimmed with red capillaries, and his pale, freckled face flushed with red-hot temper.

“Mo bean, my Woman,” he grunted at the Roman.

The Roman smirked at Liam and turned slightly to his left to the Fir Bolg leader.

“The men of this race are so ugly. Look at the face of this one. Doesn’t he look like a bleached, burned, weak, and over-washed man?”

More laughter erupted from the Fir Bolg. The Roman stroked Élan’s face, and she pulled away from his touch.

“Mo bean! My woman!” yelled Liam Ruadh, daring to push his chest into the chest of the Roman leader.

The Fir Bolg warrior pulled out his sword and held it to Liam’s throat. Liam’s eyes became thin slits of fury, and although it hurt his pride greatly, he stepped backward and turned his gaze to the stone ground. Liam's reaction gave Colm inspiration.

He thought, "This killer cares for this woman greatly. She will be my bartering piece for the truth about why he killed his fellow Celt."

"She is mine, Antonio," said Colm, looking directly at Élan to see her expression. Her eyes darted from the Roman to himself and then back to Liam. Though unfamiliar with their language, she knew she was being bartered. What she didn't know was whether she now was Fir Bolg property or belonged to the brown-skinned man.

"For now, she is yours. You might be persuaded to change your mind."

The Roman leader called out three different orders in his own tongue. Suddenly there were more strange-looking soldiers in red tunics around the Celts, and the prisoners were herded toward one of the stone buildings. Élan felt tightness around her right arm as she began to follow her tribe. She stopped and looked at her arm; the Fir Bolg warrior held a strong grasp on it.

"Sometimes the enemy is closer than you think," he said, before loosening his grip and taking a step backward from her. Liam

Ruadh immediately grabbed her left hand and pulled her away with him. She noticed that the Fir Bolg nodded in Liam's direction when he said "enemy."

Élan knew that her father had been strange in the company of Liam Ruadh ever since their night of moonlight hunting many Imbolcs ago. Liam Ruadh's hold on her hand was strong and tight and uncomfortable, but she allowed him to lead her away because he was of her tribe and would take care of her. Again she glanced behind her toward the Fir Bolg, as he stood watching her leave with Liam.

"Na bac leis an fear sin!" grunted Liam, when he turned to her and saw where her eyes were looking. "Don't bother with that man!" and he tugged her forward, dragging her even harder and with more determination.

"Liam, you are hurting my hand. Let go! I will follow without being pulled along," she said.

He looked annoyed at her assertion of independence; shades of her mother, Etain, still survived in her. He remembered how Etain had been so free within the tribe.

As the years came and went, Liam Ruadh had abandoned the older ways of thinking. The old ways that cherished women as gentle tribal leaders, in harmony with mother earth, the sacred feminine, and respected them for their life giving, were ushered out by the newer ways of the cult of the head.

Liam had a dark heart that matched the newer ways. Life-taking warriors were more esteemed, in his thinking, than feeble women. The way of the sword, the cult of the head, the brotherhood of blood; these were the principles espoused by the warrior cults.

In another time and place the Fir Bolg warrior Colm and Liam Ruadh, would have had much in common, but not now. The only thing that they both held in common right now was the truth about Diarmuid's murder.

The Irish Celts were hoarded into a stone house and motioned to sit on the floor of straw. The swords and spears held by the Roman soldiers were deterrent enough to prevent an eruption of hostility from the captives. The straw was a welcome seat and bed. Although they were hungry from their four-day excursion, thoughts of lying on a comfortable bed of straw and sleeping their fatigued bodies back to life were a better enticement than sitting up and waiting for food. Most of the group lay down to rest; others sat and talked of their future. Unsure as they were of what that was going to be, they knew that it did not mean their death. The Fir Bolg warriors could have done that four days ago at the crannog, but the captives were far more useful alive.

"What tribe are these people?" came a male voice from behind Liam.

"They do not number themselves in tribes. They are from the mainland of Europa. I have heard about their dealings with the Icinii tribes in Britannica."

"Where in Europa do they hail from, Liam?" asked Élan.

"Élan, it is nothing for you to concern yourself with," and he turned his back to answer the young man who asked the question.

"They are Romanii, from Italia, near the warmer-weathered shores that lie far south of Ireland. Beyond Gaul and Belgae."

"The Romanii are already in Britannica and are taking land from Celtic tribes like the Icinii, my father told me this…"

"Élan!" Liam's hand was at her face, and then the fingers all closed in to make a fist, his index finger pointing toward her and then coming to rest on her lips.

"Concern yourself with other things, things that do not include the matters of battles and warriors. This is talk for men."

Unaware of Liam's convictions that female warriors threatened male leadership roles, she persisted.

"My father said that the Romanii were formidable in battle. Their tactics were like nothing he has," she stopped herself and then corrected her word, "*had* seen before," remembering that Diarmuid was no longer alive.

"Did Diarmuid ever describe the tactics they used, Élan?" the young Celt asked again, waiting intently for her response. He knew how Diarmuid had raised Élan, and thought of her as having valuable opinions, not questioning her participation in the conversation.

"Tend to Grainne, she needs healing help," Liam said, pointing to a young woman who was ripping the hem of her shawl to bandage the wound on her knee. Both Élan and the young male Celt sensed Liam's displeasure over Élan's desire to continue with the conversation about Romanii warrior tactics. Élan looked at the young Celt seated behind Liam, and he just moved his shoulders up in a quiet shrug and shook his head to indicate that he did not fully understand Liam's displeasure with her involvement.

She did not move right away, but the conversation did not continue. Liam waited and stared into the green pools that seemed now to have tiny flickers of anger burning in them. Still Élan refused to move. Liam now realized that breaking her character would be more difficult than he had first thought. Her resolve was that of Etain and Diarmuid combined, an exquisite exterior and unbendable interior. She was tougher than she looked.

“No battle talk will commence until you have left our company Élan.” Liam was determined to break her. He was the warrior, the leader, the male in charge. It was not her place to lead, it was his.

“No wonder my father spoke disapprovingly of you as a tribal leader,” she said, and then continued. “The leader of the tribe hears all who wish to speak. Already you have failed as a leader, Liam!”

Élan stood up and walked away. She did not help the woman who had begun to wrap the filthy cloth from her clothing around her wounded knee. Instead she sat near the door, pulled her knees to her chest, and rested her head on her knees, tilting it to one side, watching the scene in the courtyard outside. For the first time since the day she lost her father, she cried again, silently, and missed his presence even more.

Liam continued his conversation with the younger Celt, who sat in silent shock and did not hear a word that Liam Ruadh said. Others who were seated in their vicinity also heard the altercation between Élan and Liam. As a leader Liam had failed again, as he did not have the intuition to grasp the full extent of damage done in Élan's few words. Liam was too busy relishing his conquest in conversation to recognize that he had not been communally chosen as tribal leader. His exclusion of Élan from the conversation had struck a chord among all those around him. He had not excluded Élan alone; he had excluded the valuable input of one of the most indispensable warriors, Diarmuid.

A great number of people in the tribe knew that Diarmuid had continued to train Élan by way of talk and discussion. She knew as much about the Romanii expansion in Britannica and the battles with the Icinii tribes as any male warrior. She knew of Boudicca and was inspired by the Queen's courageousness and knowledge of combat. Talk of death in war, tactics in war, and torture and humiliation in war was part of mealtime for Diarmuid and Élan. Bedtime stories were of Diarmuid's own experiences in far-off lands and of the people he had met as a young warrior. He never made his daughter feel inferior; her training was important to him. Élan knew that Diarmuid respected the ways of the tribe, but he did not respect the way that Liam Ruadh wished to rule the tribe. To Diarmuid, leadership of the tribe did not elevate the leader above other tribal members. Leadership meant standing in the middle, hearing all who wished to contribute and making a decision based on the common good.

Women and men had equal value in their contributions to discussions. Over the years with Etain, he realized that men wanted the blood of the enemy first, while women would want the blood of enemies only after discussions had failed. Peaceful negotiations almost always resulted in peace; rarely among the Celtic tribes of Ireland did violence become the solution. Diarmuid credited this to the way of women and their ability to talk evenly and without threatened tones.

The sun moved over the top of the wall, and when it had positioned itself lower in the sky, directly over the entranceway, now their prison door, Élan heard footsteps from outside. The steps grew louder and echoed in the courtyard. She lifted her head and saw the Fir Bolg warrior standing in the doorway.

Colm had not noticed her crouched in a small, lonely huddle in the shadows by the doorway. He narrowed his eyes as they adjusted to the darkness of the room. He still did not see her. The Celts barely moved to recognize the Fir Bolg's presence. Then he saw Liam Ruadh. She was not with him. The eyes glistening back from those around Liam did not resemble hers either. An unfamiliar emotion swept through the Fir Bolg, as he stood taking in all the faces in the darkness and failing to see hers. His heart actually had pain and his mind was vacant, except for thoughts of what had happened to her. Although the Fir Bolg had done many trades with the Romanii, he knew better than to trust these soldiers with a beautiful woman like Élan.

“Élan?” he called aloud, with genuine concern for her wellbeing.

It was the first time she had heard him call her name, and she was startled by it. She stood up from the shadows, about two paces behind him. He turned when he heard the straw rustling, and she emerged from the shadows. It was obvious to him that she had been crying; he smiled in relief that she was unharmed.

“Come with me,” he said, and allowed her to step toward the door before him. A shout came from the darkness.

“Élan! Do not go with him,” Liam Ruadh roared and leapt to his feet, startling those who had drifted off to sleep.

“Sit down, Liam,” she said softly. In her own mind, life as a Fir Bolg slave would fare no better than life in silence and servitude to Liam Ruadh. Her fate was ominous no matter what angle she looked at it from.

Liam was infuriated at her response and bounded toward the door to grab her, but the Fir Bolg intervened and threw his broad arm across Liam's chest, grabbing the back of his neck with the other. Liam was instantly immobilized.

"Élan and I have to discuss her father's death," the Fir Bolg whispered in Liam's ear. "When I return, you and I will discuss Diarmuid's death."

He forced Liam's face to turn toward his, and their eyes fixed on each other. Liam knew that the truth was about to surface about Diarmuid. He was helpless to prevent the Fir Bolg from telling Élan about it. Unsure how much the Fir Bolg had seen, he felt confident that as a negotiator he could manipulate the talks and make himself the hero. He nodded in agreement with the Fir Bolg and felt the tense grip on the back of his neck slowly release.

"Go sit back down. I will return shortly."

Liam looked at Élan; her stare was empty, devoid of hope. The dismantling of her way of thinking had already begun: First despair, then acceptance. Liam was determined to make her succumb to his rules.

"I will not turn my back on you, Irish Celt, until you return to where you were seated," replied the Fir Bolg. "If Liam had no reservations about killing his own tribesman, he certainly would not think twice about stabbing an enemy in the back," thought Colm. Liam again nodded and turned to walk back into the shadows, to the place where he had been seated.

"The Romanii will bring you food shortly, and then you will be locked in for the night. The guards by the gate will be there always. Your fates will be decided tonight, and tomorrow some of you will stay here at Dromanagh fort. The others will travel with me, back to Belgae. Be happy you are all still alive."

Élan and the Fir Bolg walked out into the courtyard. When their footfalls became faint and distant, the group discussion began again with Liam in the leadership role. His words neither gave hope nor assured the Irish Celts of their safety. They wondered if they would ever see Élan again and if they would remain at this fort or be dragged to Belgae. Nobody's input was heeded as Liam talked on about overtaking the two soldiers by the gate and escaping the Roman fortress at night. Liam, unable to instill hope, unable to activate the group with rousing words, left most of the Irish Celts accepting their captivity and disregarding Liam as a leader. Liam, irate at the lack of responsiveness, grabbed the young Celt behind him and pulled him closer.

"Are you with me?" he yelled into the young man's face. The group now understood that Liam Ruadh was an unstable leader.

The chieftain, feeble, old, and sick, had held onto his role longer than was normal within a tribe, and now they all knew why. He was waiting for a more stable leader to emerge from the ranks of the tribe. And emerging she was, for it was with the chieftain's full knowledge and blessing that Diarmuid had trained Élan. The transition would have needed to take place slowly, as Liam had a sufficient following to cause the tribe to divide over an issue such as leadership.

Liam was a good negotiator, but the chieftain also saw him as rash and unfair, two qualities that, no matter how hard the chieftain tried to educate Liam, he held onto with tenacity and stubbornness.

Élan was the chieftain's next replacement. He was just waiting for time to pass and for Liam to reveal himself as a poor choice as a leader. His plan did not evolve because of the Fir Bolg invasion and his death. Élan was to learn of her leadership role from her father and the chieftain on her eighteenth Imbolc. Now she would possibly never learn of it at all. Both men were dead, but Grainne was still alive, and was one of the twenty-three brought to Dromanagh.

As Élan strode beside the Fir Bolg, she felt weary and bleak. Then she remembered her own shock at hearing the Fir Bolg call her by name. She even remembered the emotion in his voice when he said it.

“Why were you suddenly concerned for my well-being?’ she asked, looking up to see if she could detect any feelings in his features.
“The enemy was closer than you thought,” he responded flatly, in a matter-of-fact voice.

“You said that when we were being brought to the stone house. What do you mean by that?” Her strides became unnaturally longer to keep up with his pace.

“What do you know of your tribesman Liam? You seemed to think both he and your father were close when we met some days ago.”

“Well, first…we did not just ‘meet’ some days ago. If my memory serves me well, you and your men forced your way into our crannog, killed the chieftain and my father…”

“Now that is where your memory serves you poorly,” he interrupted.

“You killed the chieftain and my father, I saw it with my own eyes!” she exclaimed in disbelief. Her body was now in front of him, her hands on her hips and her green eyes burning through him.

“Tell me what you saw with your eyes, and I will then tell you what I saw with mine,” the Fir Bolg warrior replied, amazed at her boldness toward him. He found this an attractive characteristic.

“You’re smiling at me. Don’t do that,” Élan said, as she lowered her eyes and abruptly looked away from him. He roped her arm through his and responded in a mocking tone.

“My apologies, Élan, I swear never to smile at you again, unless of course you change that ruling.”

This time she did not fight back, for it dawned on her that she was being awarded more respect from this enemy than from her own tribesman Liam. She was not to be won over that easily, though. Colm felt her pull away from him, and he looped his arm through hers even tighter now, and halted in his step. He turned her toward his face so he could see her reaction.

“The enemy is closer than you think. Do you understand what I mean?”

"No, I do not understand what you mean," she responded, with utter dismay. Who was this enemy? Was it him or someone in the settlement, or even one of his own tribesmen? Élan was completely confused now.

"Are you telling me we are all in danger here, and if so, why did you bring us here with you? Are we slaves for you to barter with? Are we in danger of losing our lives?"

He tried to interrupt her bantering and sensed she was becoming angrier and angrier, which she was. So Colm Riordán, the fierce Fir Bolg Celtic warrior, braced himself, for he knew that fury was on its way.

"You stole us from the only home we have ever known!" She swung her free arm around and thumped him in the middle of his chest. He stood there and took it quietly.

"You killed my father!" Again a huge thump landed solidly on his chest. His upper torso rocked minutely, and he remained silent. She was about to swing again and land a solid third thump, when she realized he was not doing anything to stop her, though he could easily have overpowered her. Colm stood, arms dangling by his sides, ready to receive her blows, but doing nothing to fight her off.

“I was the enemy. I did steal you away from your crannog, but Élan, please believe me when I tell you, my hands were not on my knife when it stabbed your father.”

She stood away from him, and her gaze moved from her hand, on his chest for strike number three, up to his eyes. They had softened and lost their coldness. Élan stepped away and shook her head in disbelief.

“No. I saw what happened.”

“What did you see?” Colm asked, and then gently reminded her. “Think of where you were standing, where I was, where your father stood, and then try to remember where your tribesman Liam Ruadh was standing.”

Her brow began to furrow deeply as she whisked herself back in her mind to the scene on that terrible day.

The crannog gate was blocked by the Fir Bolgs on their horses. “You and your men had just entered the crannog on horseback.”

“Yes, where were your father and Liam standing?”

“They stood together in the crowd, watching.”

"When I greeted your father, where were you?" Colm asked trying to help her remember the scene.

"I was still near the crannog gate; my father motioned to me to stay where I was as you made your way through the crowd in the crannog."

"When I greeted your father, Élan…try to remember, because this is all I have to prove to you that I am no longer the enemy…where and how did we stand?"

"You both were holding each other by the elbows, you embraced and spoke to each other, but I was too far away to hear what was being said."

"Élan, your father and I knew each other, we embraced, and we still held each other by the arms when he was stabbed. Now try to remember…who shouted 'Dagger!' and where was that person standing?"

"Liam was near both of you, but he had no reason to kill my father. They were tribesmen."

"My hands had no blood when your father fell to the ground, and Liam was covered in blood. He killed your father, but I do not know why." Colm waited for the roars of "Liar!" but they did not come.

“Do you believe me?” he asked, astonished at how calmly she was accepting his account of what had happened.

“Liam Ruadh killed my father?” she responded, in a shocked and slightly questioning tone. “I…I don’t understand why he would have done that.”

“I think I have figured out a way to get him to confess, but I need you to trust me and help me.”

“I don’t know,” she replied. “You are asking me to believe that a tribesman killed my father and to trust you, the man who ransacked our crannog and destroyed our way of life. Why should I trust you and not him?” The anger in her voice was so vivid it spiced every word that spit out.

“Because I know you saw no blood on my hands.” Colm was eager to make her remember the events of the day with clarity. “If only she could put things in order,” he thought, “this would make sense to her.”

“No, no, you do not know that.” She shook her head, and the furrow returned to her brow.

"Yes, Élan, I do know that. Remember more of what happened that day…you fainted."

"Yes, I woke up and realized I was being carried by you on your horse."
"Was your clothing stained in blood?"

"No, this is what I wore that day." Her dress was soiled with grass and mud, but there was no blood.

"Was Liam unstained, Élan?"

Her face lost all color, her green eyes narrowed, and she stared off into the distance behind Colm at nothing in particular. Her mind had transported her back to the top of Colm's horse; she saw Liam ahead of them and that when he turned he was covered in blood.

"He was covered in blood," she said, in a half-dreamy and half-awake state.

"What about my clothes? Were they stained?"

Again she was transported back mentally to the top of Colm's horse. "You smelled of perfume, freshness, and salt."

Élan looked into Colm's face.

"But he was helping my father, which is why he was covered in blood."

"No, Élan, he had blood on his hands *before* your father fell to the ground. It was Liam Ruadh who held my dagger and stabbed your father. The dagger never left my leather belt; he stabbed your father when I tried to embrace him in thanks for saving my life many years ago."

"My father saved your life?" she asked incredulously. "You and he knew each other?" Again she shook her head; this was too much to believe.

"I recognized him, and then when I saw this wristlet, I knew it was the same man."

Colm bent his arm up and took the wristlet off. "Your father told me that his wife gave him this wristlet with the symbol of the triune goddess of birth, life, and death when he and your mother spent their first night together. Many years ago he and I met in battle on the southern coast of Ireland. He severely wounded me, was about to kill me, when I grabbed his arm. I touched this wristlet and asked him to leave me wounded but not to leave me dead."

"You are the Belgae that he told me about?" It was as if a ghost from her father's past had appeared in front of her. "You are the warrior he walked away from, never to kill another?"
"He spoke of me to you?" Colm asked, relieved that the wristlet was convincing her of his innocence. He looked toward the ground and shook his head in true sorrow.

"I did not kill your father, Élan. He was the finest man I have ever met. He spared my life. I never took heed of his words; I was raised and trained to be a warrior. I had no choice in the matter."

Here his voice cracked. Colm Riordán was remembering all the men he had killed, all the lives he had ended, and he was swamped in regret. He couldn't change all of that now; he realized it was part of his own unchangeable history.

Élan nodded. "My mother told my father that the young Belgae he met on the shores of Corcaigh that winter was a sign for my father that the warrior life was unfulfilling. He described the event as a release from captivity. He never killed a man again after that day. It gave him power to give you your life."

"Do you believe me now that I did not kill your father?" He held her hand and draped the wristlet into it.

"Yes. I believe you." Élan took the wristlet, and Colm tied it around her arm. She touched it, felt the three intertwined leaves, and shook her head. Then she looked up at Colm. Her face, sad and pensive, Colm knew that she was in shock. Liam had killed her father, and she was sure of it now.

"The Romans are a very clean race, you know? Let's get you all cleaned up and ready for some food," Colm said, as he nodded in relief that she now believed him.

"What about the others?" Her voice was far away, her eyes a blank stare.

"They will get cleaned and ready for food, too. Tonight you will dine with me and then return to them, if you wish?"

Élan shook her head.

"No, Colm Riordan. I will eat with my tribesmen. I am not a Fir Bolg, I never will be. I cannot abandon my tribesmen…, and I won't."

Colm blinked and pursed his lips tightly as he nodded.

"I promised your father I would save you and keep you free."

"What will happen to the others?" she asked again, almost afraid to hear the answer.

“They will be transported to great estates and empires throughout Europa and become servants.” He knew his answer was pathetic and selfish.

“Then I, too, will be transported with them. My father may have wished for my freedom, Colm, but he himself would not have abandoned his tribesmen, and neither will I.”
“I need to fix this,” he said with regret.

“Let them keep Liam Ruadh. The others must be returned to the crannog.”

“They won’t let us leave with you.” He knew the conversation was far from being over.

“You are a good man in the depths of your soul; I know this to be true of you. There are women and boys back in that stone hut, weary, lonely, and afraid for their lives. I cannot leave them to be free by myself, knowing that they face captivity forever.”

“Élan, I cannot change this. It cannot be undone now,” Colm said, as he grasped his head in his hands and pulled at his jawline in frustration.

“Remember that to give life is far more powerful than to take it. You ask me to go with you and become clean and eat while my tribesmen sit in filth and are hungry. This is impossible. I ask you to free all but one, and you say this is impossible." She held his hands to her face and said, "These things we ask of each other can be done, but we both must help the other to achieve them."

"How, Élan? The Romans have counted twenty-three servants. I have told them that you are mine. They have twenty-two to trade with. How can I undo what is done? The settlement is secure and guarded." His warrior mind wanted to kill five thousand Roman men, women, and children and lead Élan and her twenty-one tribesmen back to freedom.

Élan's mind worked in a different way. No killing, no fighting, no intimidating war-like tactics were needed to execute her plan.

"Tell them we are diseased. It is spreading rapidly, and it kills quickly." Her answer was swift and delivered with clarity.

"What ailment makes you glow rosy, look healthy and gives you an appetite? You were all healthy when the Roman observed you earlier." Colm grinned at her rapid speech and racing thoughts, but then realized that her plan might indeed work.

“Flowers.” Élan was staring at the field leading down to the shore of Loughshinny.

“Flowers?” Colm laughed. “Eat with me tonight. We will discuss this further.” He wanted nothing more than to stay transfixed and relaxed in her presence. She was exciting and calming all at once. “Your great plan will work, but it needs more discussion.”

Élan smiled and nodded, and they walked side by side to his stone dwelling. There she washed and changed into the Roman garments females wore at that time.

When she emerged from the room bathed and dressed all in white robes, Colm realized that she was by far the most beautiful woman he had ever seen. The fact that she was unaware and unassuming of how beautiful she truly was, made her even more beautiful.
Her loose brunette hair fell in bundles of careless waves and draped easily over her shoulders and down her back. Colm tried hard not to keep looking, but this was a difficult task.

The Romans had brought food such as bread and cooked meat, and the table had been decorated with dried local flowers—foxgloves, red poppies, and beautifully dried white sprays of clematis.

Élan sat at the table, picked up a clematis spray, and smelled it. She swirled it gently in her hand and placed it back on the table. She bit her bottom lip and looked at Colm. Then she took a sprig of foxglove and pressed the dried buds into her hands, rubbing them together, making the buds into a powder.

"That will stop the itch," she said. "Would you like to hear my plan now, Colm?' she asked, as she watched him walk over to the table toward her. He sat beside her, and she could see that his mind was far away.

It was the same look her father wore when haunted by the spirits of all the people he had killed. She knew that, like Diarmuid, Colm would sit up many nights, and for many years to come, seeing the faces of the dead he had left behind on the battlefield. Night after night, especially in winter, Diarmuid lay sleepless, finally giving in and sitting up. It was on one of these nights that she awoke and asked her father what was the matter. In his wide-eyed fatigue, it was Etain's voice that spoke to him, not his daughter's, and he answered absentmindedly and truthfully.

"I have killed so many men, so many. I see their faces when I lie down and close my eyes. They haunt me." And staring out into the darkness beyond the door of his hut, he imagined an eternity in the nowhere. "I wish I could change it all, take it back. But I can't. My spirit is destroyed."

"How many men have you killed, Father?" This time it was Élan's voice he heard, not Etain's. And Diarmuid was ashamed that his daughter now knew he was a killer of men.

As Élan watched Colm's face grow dark with hopelessness, she repeated now what her father had said that night so long ago.

"It doesn't matter if it was one or one thousand lives, you can't change the past." Colm's stare now came to her face.

"How can one so young be so wise?" he asked her.

"What you can change, Colm, is the present. Help me get these Irish Celts back home?"

He nodded and replied "yes" so quietly that he seemed to her to be a different man than the monster who invaded the crannog.

"And the reason I am so wise, as you call it, is because I had a father who was a warrior, and he too lamented all that he had done. These feelings will come and go. The spirits of the dead will not let you rest. But if you keep killing, the destruction to yourself is certain. Let the spirits haunt you. They deserve it, and so do you. Now we move forward."

"I am sorry," he said.

"Do you want to hear my plan, Colm?" she asked, staring at his face and measuring the emotion in it.

"Yes," he answered, dividing up the food before them.

"Don't touch those dried flowers," she added. "We are going to need them later."

Élan smiled as she imagined the Romanii picking the clematis and witches' gloves and poppies in the summer, drying them in bundles hanging upside down in some dark corner of the kitchen. She giggled and shook her head in disbelief, envisioning beautiful Romanii women in their robes of white, itching the palms of their hands and their forearms.

"I wonder if they understood why they itched so much after collecting the flowers?" she said out loud, in distraction.
"Why they itched?" Colm asked, struggling to tear meat away from the bone with his teeth.

"Yes, the servants. They must have never realized that the clematis was a toxic plant. Unless, of course, they counteracted its effect by gathering witches' gloves at the same time!"

"Please explain your Irish Celtic language to me. I have not understood one word," Colm said leaning his elbow on his bent knee and holding the leg of cooked pheasant aloft like a victory banner.

“Only if you share that with me,” she said reaching for the meat.

Chapter 8

Despite the fact that Mona was a very-well-preserved bog body, time had ravaged certain aspects of her face. The sheer weight of the bog had distorted her features. It was possible to tell her eye color, and hair color, and by doubling the length of her arm span, the forensic scientists could give a good guess as to how tall she was.

In today's world, Mona would have been a green eyed brunette, five feet six inches in height, and of slender build. The radio-carbon 14 dating of the sally rod in her ankle had placed her age as that of a true Iron Age bog body. The CAT scan revealed that her body had been pregnant at the time of death.

As always, Maire was the first to arrive in the Museum lab where Mona was kept. The case seemed to have been solved by forensic science. Radio-carbon dating of bone taken from Mona's ankle revealed that she died around 700 BC. X-Ray fluorescence tests showed that the metals in parts of the torc around Mona's neck were forged in or around 700 BC. The special bio-archaeologist that flew in from Scotland's

University of Glasgow had determined, from an eight-inch strand of hair taken from Mona's head, that she had died in winter, basing his findings on the large amount of proteins that were visible toward the root area of the strand under an electron microscope. Winter would have been a time for consumption of meat and not grains. Winter was also declared to be the season of demise based on the tests completed on Mona's fingernails. The chemical composition was very high in nitrogen, which also explained the perfect preservation of the body.

The lack of striations on the fingernails when they were studied under a microscope further revealed that Mona did not do physically hard work or labor. Indeed, it seemed to the specialist from Glasgow that Mona had been accustomed to getting Celtic manicures of sorts. It was also this same bio-archaeologist who discovered that Mona's hair had been styled with vegetable plant oil and a resin combination that grew only in France or Spain. He also revealed that Mona's red hair was bleached lighter with the use of lime. Her bodily hair was darker.

The hair on her head was exceptionally well preserved because of the lime, and the lime lightened her hair to its existing color. With further chemical testing on another strand, he determined that she was a brunette prior to bleaching her hair.

Still, there were parts that did not quite fit together neatly. The CT scan showed disks in her stomach but did not show clearly what these disks were. Both Maire and Sean desperately wanted to know and had petitioned the Museum board for permission to open Mona's stomach and get the answer to their question. This was the day to reveal that answer. After today, Mona would be freeze-dried and stored in the Museum for occasional display to the public and now and again brought to the lab for maintenance and further study. Her skin would not be as supple after the freeze drying process. Her features would also distort a little more. So 3-D imaging, completion of a clay model of her face, and an autopsy would be her last big adventures.

As far as Sean was concerned, the day of the autopsy was approaching about as fast as a snail on the sticky side of adhesive tape. Maire reminded Sean on more than one occasion that waiting for the day to arrive was like waiting for Santa to come. Most food would have been destroyed by stomach acid, so chances were, the disks were definitely not food. Whatever they were, they would last a few weeks more. They had already lasted two thousand years.

When the day finally did arrive, Sean was in the lab before Maire, a highly unusual and, most likely, never-to-be-repeated event. A quick stop at the local chemist to pick up her prescription pills put Maire behind schedule. Six months of taking the pills had left her moody, emotional, and just plain crabby, but not pregnant. Rory was not a happy camper, and she wasn't too sure how she felt. She removed the pills from the box, popped one into her mouth, washed it down with a gulp of coffee, and shoved the packet of white pills into the top pocket of her denim jacket. This stop had put her behind schedule on a very important day.

"Agghhh!" she wailed, as she dodged cars and buses, desperate to get to the lab, and feeling the side effects already. When she arrived at the museum, Sean was waiting for her.

The area had to be fully prepped, and when it was, they both looked at each other and nodded. Then Sean burst into "It's now or never!" with gusto and enthusiasm. At this point in their work relationship, Maire realized that Sean used humor to disguise nervous energy.

Just as Sean was serenading Maire with "Be mine tonight," the gurney's end pushed through the double doors, with the museum's custodian of antiquities dressed in a green surgical gown struggling at the other end.

"Morning, Sean, Maire."

He was a man in his early sixties with gray fly-away hair that, when coupled with the green Johnny coat, gave him the air of a mad scientist.

“She’s set to go,” he said in his soft south side Dublin accent. “Thanks, Mr. Martin,” Maire responded, guiding the gurney beneath the bright lights.

“Listen, Maire,” he said, as he handed over the gurney to her. “At some point I would like to talk to you about the location where the body was discovered. I think it might be of great interest to you and might contribute to the reason she was so badly tortured before she died.”
“I would love to get some more information about that,” Maire answered. “I should be finished here in about an hour. Will you be in your office then?” she asked, removing the sheet carefully.

“Fine. That’ll be fine. I’ll see you in my office in an hour.”

“Can I come too?’ asked Sean, feeling a little abandoned.

“Of course! It will interest the two of you greatly.” With a small wave he turned and padded softly back out the double doors and down the hall.

"Well, I for one am greatly intrigued." Sean looked at Maire to see if she had a clue as to what Mr. Martin would have to say.

"No clue?" he asked, hitting a high pitch on the word "clue."

Maire stretched her lips into a downward bow and furrowed her brow.

"No," she said, shaking her head and shrugging her shoulders. "Let's get started, shall we?"

They took their positions on either side of Mona. The lab was ready for the autopsy, and both Maire and Sean would do the job, with Maire in the lead, as it was still her gig.

The blue Touch 'n Tough surgical examination gloves were pulled on, and the scalpel sliced through the leathery abdominal cavity with some resistance. Maire applied a bit more pressure, and the slit revealed the shrunken brownish organs inside. When the disks were taken from Mona's stomach, Sean was more perplexed than ever.

Although the coins had been attacked severely by stomach acid some of the surfaces were ravaged, and the relief of the pictures and scenes had flattened, Sean immediately recognized one with

"Romulus" in Roman letters and seven hills below the lettering of the name.

"That's impossible," he said in astonishment. "I—it just—it doesn't make any sense."

To Maire, who was not a student of Latin, the letters meant nothing to her.

"What doesn't make sense? We don't even know what these disks are, Sean, of course, nothing makes sense!"

"Oh, I know what these disks are, thanks to the Jesuits, and when I tell you what they are, it will make even less sense to you."

"Okay, you have my full attention," she said pulling herself to a standing position and standing with the scalpel in her right hand.

"Go ahead, astound me with your knowledge of Celtic history Professor Sullivan."

"Actually," Sean replied dryly, "this has nothing to do with Celtic history." He held up the coin that had been the best preserved and showed the visible lettering and relief.

"This here, Maire, is a Roman coin."
"What the hell are you on about?" she said, tired and growing increasingly impatient with Sean, or was it the effects of her pills again? She couldn't decide.

"I am telling you that this is a Roman coin, Maire! No joking!" Sean was not in the mood to spend a lengthy period of time trying to convince her about this. The oddness of finding a Roman coin inside the stomach of an Iron Age Irish bog body was upsetting to him. It was usually at this stage of the investigation and research that they were drawing to a close and the pieces were beginning to all fit together. These coins just opened up a whole new can of worms.

"The lettering and relief show that this coin is dedicated to Romulus of the seven hills."

"Of Rome?" she asked in utter disbelief.

"Of Rome." He nodded and then shook his head in total and utter disbelief.
"What the hell is she doing with Roman coins in her stomach?" Maire was indeed even more baffled than before. "Did Romulus even exist as early as she did?"

"He founded Rome by populating five out of the seven hills and elected one hundred patricians to serve in the first Roman senate. This, supposedly, happened in 753 BC," Sean recited automatically. Sean was most definitely a history nerd.

Maire stared at him blankly. "You're a nerd!" Then, "You're having me on, Sean!" her delayed response.

"I love history, Maire," he smiled his huge, gloating smile. "No, I am not having you on, or shitting you, or joking you, or pulling your leg even." He pulled the coin closer to his eyes and squinted to sharpen his vision.

"Let me see it please Sean?" She held one of the best preserved disks.

"We probably could do x-ray fluorescence testing to see when the metals were forged, right? Like we did on the torc?" She was not asking, she was going to go ahead and do it any way.

"I'll let you think out loud but I'll continue to stick to my guns and place a bet with you that these coins were forged in or around 700 BC, which, in case you've forgotten, is how old Mona is."

"Why would she have Roman coins in her stomach?" Maire, no longer listening to Sean's banter, pulled the coin closer to her eye, and examined it from every possible angle.

"Let's finish this up. We'll do the x-ray testing after we get Mona sorted out. Twenty Euros says I am right about the date the coins were minted, though," Sean said.
Maire sighed and stood back from the gurney looking at Mona.

"This is it for her. I'm relieved that she is finally done with all of the testing and examinations. I felt all along that she wasn't a bog body at all, Sean. I wanted to solve the whole thing about how she died and why, but I don't think it's going to happen. Do you know what I mean?"

Though she was sad that her time with Mona the bog body was over, she knew that, realistically, Mona's story would only be partially revealed.

"We need to invent a time machine, Sean."

"I'll get right onto it, Master," Sean responded in his best Igor voice.

"Seriously, though, I know what you mean," Sean said, with surprising candor, slipping the Roman coins into a plastic storage bag and putting them into his left front pocket.

"I felt myself that we were solving a very recent, intricate and messy murder. But you know Maire; I don't think we are any closer to solving this thing."

"If they do decide to put Mona on display, I would like to request that her clothing be replaced and she be displayed gracefully. Not like the way she was buried."
"Agreed," Sean said. "She's been through enough, so it is time to let her rest in peace."

"Let's give her back her dignity," Maire said, already setting to work.

It only took about fifteen minutes to restore Mona to her original state. The skin was glued back together. The sheet was replaced and the touch 'n' tough gloves discarded. They both began to guide the gurney toward the double doors.

"Let's get her back to Martin and listen to what he has to say about the bog she was found in," Sean said, motioning with his head for Maire to hold the double doors open as he guided the gurney back down the hallway to the office of the Custodian of Museum Antiquities.

Martin was seated at his desk with a large magnifying glass and the brightest desk light shining onto a very large and very old map. He stood up when they knocked at the door.

“Come in,” he said. “Sit down there while I put Mona.., it is Mona?” they both nodded, “into the climate control chamber.” They sat down on creaky old oak chairs. Sean stretched his legs out in front of him and his arms back behind him, touching a glass vase by accident and causing it to rock.
“Oh, shit!” he said grabbing it in both hands whilst leaning backward and almost doing a back flip out of the chair. As Martin walked back in, Sean was in mid flip and holding the glass vase. Martin walked behind Sean, took the vase gently from him, and placed it on a higher shelf. Eying Sean, he gave a slightly dissatisfied cough, then sniffed in disgust and methodically made his way to his own desk, repositioning himself over the ancient map. Martin’s lecture began.

“Most people today think that the borders of counties and provinces in Ireland were the same during the age of the Celts. Some are; for example, Ulster, Munster, Leinster, and Connaught, are still the provinces. And their Celtic qualities are still known among scholars as war, music, prosperity, and knowledge, respectively, and of course their elements too —, earth, fire, air, and water."

Maire and Sean both wondered if, and how, this information pertained to Mona. Oblivious to the darting looks behind his back, Martin continued on.

"However, unlike today, in Iron Age Ireland, geographically there are thought to have been five provinces, not four." Suddenly reanimated and interested, Sean chimed in, "Meath," and nodded, knowing he was right.

"Meath, indeed," came Martin's response.

-"Which means that current borders of provinces are different than in Iron Age times," Sean added, with certainty, but still unsure, though, where Martin was leading the conversation.

"When we take a look at this ancient map of all five provinces, Ulster, Munster, Leinster, Connaught, and Meath, also referred to as Middle Ground, Boteen's bog, and more precisely, the actual spot where the body was found, is on the exact ancient border of Connaught, Meath, and Munster."

The two archaeologists rose immediately and bent more deeply over the map.

“Show me where she would have been buried,” Maire said to Martin, somehow knowing that this was significant, but unable to determine how.

“Here,” Martin pointed and raised his position in the chair so as to better his view of the map.

“Here is what we call Eber’s Half of Ireland; part of the legendary division between Heremeon’s half, Ir’s corner, Eber’s half, and Lughaid’s corner. This is all based on Celtic myth now, mind you, but actual burial sites, existence of Forts, and various finds that suggest places of dwelling all lend themselves to the firm belief that this very spot here.” Again he pointed to the north shores of Lough Derg, but more toward Offaly and Tipperary and more central. – “Right here, is in neither one county nor kingdom nor tribal dwelling. This was no-man’s land, so to speak.”

“Interesting,” Maire said. “You must have a theory about why this is significant as to *why* she was buried there?” Maire added and stood back to take in his features. His brow became animated as he spoke, and the mad scientist look took over.

“I do indeed, Maire.”

"I'd love to hear about it, Mr. Martin," she said, now even more interested than before. Even Sean stopped looking at the map and brought Martin into his line of vision, as he stepped beside Maire.

"I have been custodian or curator of museum antiquities here since 1979. That is twenty-five years. Among all the remains and bog bodies discovered in those twenty-five years all of them, I emphasize *all of them*, were found on old tribal borders. The Celts had a belief in the afterlife..., —they called it the other world, correct?"

Both Sean and Maire nodded in agreement. Martin continued on.

"Revered Celts were buried with artifacts that would help them on their journey to the other world. Victims of sacrificial killing were not. They had only the clothes on their backs. Only Sacrificial bog bodies were buried on tribal borders. All other bodies were buried in solid ground and in ornate, well-stocked graves. The sacrificial bodies were always in bogs. In Iron age, times these bogs would have been swampy, mystical-pools of water, like bottomless pits."

Again the two silent listeners nodded in agreement.

"I have always thought that on occasion the rituals used in sacrificial killings would help to solve the puzzle of whether or not these people went to death willingly, for the appeasement of their gods. Take a look at the last two bog bodies found in Ireland, Clony Cavan Man and Old Croghan Man."

Martin now produced photographs of the two bog bodies he spoke of as they were exhumed from the bogs. He continued on as Sean and Maire listened intently. Although both were still not quite sure how this pertained to Mona, they were interested.

"Both Clony Cavan and Old Croghan were dismembered and generally tortured, in keeping with older discoveries, such as Lindow Man, Gallagh Man, and Tollund Man. Their blows were all leading to a final, fatal blow that would kill them." He pointed to detailed pictures of the bodies showing their wounds and the fatal blows.
Then Martin pulled out Mona's file. He opened it and lined up all the detailed photographs of her wounds and, lashes, the sally rod puncture wounds, and the indentation of the torc on her neck.

"Your bog body has not one fatal blow. She was tortured and then choked to death on peat, the Golden Orb, and even more peat. She was not a sacrifice. I firmly believe she was a murder victim. Even her place of burial suggests that her spirit had to be

trapped in a nowhere existence: Neither on land nor in water, but in a swamp; Neither in one tribal kingdom nor another, but on the border. She was being punished."
"For what?" Maire asked, looking at him, her eyes big as saucers.

"I don't know. Maybe for those Roman coins you found in her stomach," Martin said, collecting all the pictures and stacking them back into their files.

"How did you know about the coins?" Sean asked, pulling out the plastic bag of coins and marveling at Martin's great guesswork.
Martin shuffled in his seat a little before answering in an uncharacteristically awkward way.

- "I saw them in the plastic storage bag in your hand when you were juggling with my glass vase over there."

"Oh," Sean said, feeling stupid. "Yes…,- am…,- sorry."

"Thanks for taking the time to explain all of this to us," Maire said, sensing a growing uneasiness between Martin and Sean. "This will be a great help to us tomorrow. She was definitely not a sacrifice, especially when you consider that she was also pregnant when she was killed."

Martin nodded and began to roll up the map.

"If we need to have a look at the map again, can we?" she asked, before turning to leave.
"Certainly," and then Martin added a light hearted, "Good luck tomorrow."

"That was amazing," Sean said.

"Yes, it was," she said. "But do you know what was even more amazing, Sean?"

"No. What?" he asked.

"Martin has x-ray vision."

"What the hell are ya on about?" Sean said, a loud guffaw rattling against the bare hallway walls.

"Well," Maire said, in a droll tone, "he could look right into the left front pocket of your trousers."

"You are talking shite now," Sean said, eyeing her sideways, looking slightly demented. -"You've gone mad. You're officially a mad scientist!"

“Oh, am I now?” Maire asked, pushing through the doorway back into the brightly lit lab.

“How is it, then, that he knew about the Roman coins when you had put them into a plastic storage bag and then into your left front pocket before you even began to wheel the gurney out of this room?”

Sean reached into his left front pants pocket and drew out the coins in the plastic bag. “I never had them in my hands when I was trying to catch the bloody glass vase, did I? How the hell did he know?”

“He’s hiding something, Sean. He knows more than he is telling us.”

“Agreed.” They both looked at each other and just shook their heads.

“Let’s work on getting all this information together for the presentation tomorrow,” she added, heading toward the paper-filled desk at the right of the room.

***

That night, at home, Maire obsessed over Martin and the Roman coins. She did some laundry and folded clothes. It wasn’t until

she opened the washing machine door that she noticed the white powdery dust, soggy and sticky, everywhere.
"What the…—?" She held up her denim jacket and heard the crinkle of plastic and foil in the top left-hand pocket.

"The pills!"

She remembered putting her prescription pills into her denim jacket pocket earlier that morning, and the white sticky powder was explained away.

She felt relieved; relieved that she had unknowingly destroyed her month's prescription of pills, the same pills that would help her to get pregnant. She knew that this emotion was not in keeping with what she should be feeling if she truly wanted to be pregnant. Leaning against the machine, she shook her head and cried. Two emotions enveloped her at once —, relief and guilt— relief that she had finally come to a decision about getting pregnant, and guilt that she did not want to be a mother.

Instead of calling in another prescription, she went upstairs, opened the medicine cabinet in her bathroom, and took out a packet of contraceptive pills. She checked the expiration date; they were still good. In case the polycystic ovarian syndrome had been cleared up in the course of the six months, she wanted to make sure that getting pregnant was still out of the question.

The decision made, she popped a contraceptive pill into her mouth and washed it down with a glass of water. Eyeing herself in the mirror, Maire saw that for the first time in months, maybe even years, she knew who she was, and she was ok with it.

It had been six months since Maire Moylan had been delivered to Booteen's bog in North Tipperary by helicopter. The excitement of the discovery that day had waned and was replaced by perplexing questions. Forensic science revealed many truths but failed to reveal the big truth—, why Mona was murdered.

Many notable historians of Celtic bog bodies had come and talked to Maire and Sean over the last six months. They had examined Mona, -her clothing, and the outcomes of all testing, and then each had formulated their own theories.

The three most prominent Celtic historians disagreed amongst themselves. No one could agree on whether or not Mona was a ritualistic sacrifice, a criminal undergoing capital punishment, or a murder victim.

The Roman coins in her stomach perplexed everyone. Was she forced to swallow them, smuggling them? It was any one's guess really. But as Sean had predicted, the coins were indeed Roman and were forged in or around 700 BC. The x-ray fluorescence testing of the coins proved it. He demanded his twenty Euros from Maire, and she handed the money over promptly.

Mona had revealed her last meal, the time of year she died, her age, her status in the Celtic Tribe, even her true hair color. Only guessing games could be played as to why she had three Roman coins in her stomach.

The 3-D computer imaging became an eerie experience for Maire and Sean. The computer imaging specialist had notified them that his mission was completed and that they would be able to see the final 3-D computer image on Wednesday at three in the afternoon.

The designated time arrived, and Maire and Sean stood limp and quiet behind the seated computer imaging specialist. Mona's facial skeletal structure built itself together on the computer screen, all the while turning in a full 360-degree circle. With each revolution of the skull, new muscles, and then the skin, hair, eyes, and lips appeared. When the layering of Mona's face was complete, a woman with large green eyes, pale skin, and straight brunette hair stared back at them from the computer screen.

"This is what your Iron Age woman would have looked like."

“She is beautiful.” Sean said and then he looked at Maire to see her reaction.

She stared at the image on the screen. Finally, she saw the human being, the person. Mona had never been just a bog body to Maire; she had always been a person.

“My God,” she responded. “She is beautiful. God help her. She was tortured beyond belief.”

“When are you meeting with the board to discuss your findings?” the computer specialist asked, as he began burning the graphics to a disk.

“Tomorrow morning at nine,” Maire replied. “Thanks a million for giving her a face. Amazing stuff, really.”

-“We will provide the sculptor of the clay model of the face with this disk so he can get started on his job. How are they planning on displaying her?” the 3D imaging specialist asked, writing “Booteen’s Bog Woman” on the disk and placing it into a clear plastic jewel case.

“We don’t know yet. We will be meeting with the board of directors tomorrow and will report our findings to them. I’ll ask what they are planning to do.”

Maire took one last look at the green-eyed brunette doing 360-degree revolutions on the computer screen and again shook her head gently.

"Amazing," Maire said, her voice a soft whisper.

At nine the next morning Maire and Sean brought their findings and presentation into the meeting room for the national museum's board of directors. The bog body find had made headlines six months ago and then faded away. There had been a number of these finds throughout Ireland over the last three decades. What the media and the public did not know was that this find differed greatly from all the others, in a variety of ways. Even if the public had been made aware, Maire was certain that very few people would appreciate Mona because of these subtle differences as much as she and Sean did.

Sean and Maire stood side by side at the large mahogany table. There were five board members present and eager to hear what Maire and Sean had learned.

The lap top was connected to the overhead screen, and Sean and Maire began the presentation, pictures appearing behind them on a screen.

The first pictures were of Mona's body being exhumed from the bog, from the foot protruding from the sod to the slow reveal of a fully clothed pregnant body buried upside down. Full facial pictures showed that the oral cavity was forced wide open with sod. The early pictures showed the torc embedded into the neck and the sally rod forced through the ankles. For each picture, Maire spoke precisely about on-site findings and the condition of the body.

The lab pictures revealed the golden orb in the throat and the torc indentations of the ornate deer head in the neck of the bog body. The perfect decoration of the tunic and the amount of detail in the trim were highlighted in the pictures. Maire presented the facts and findings to the board, using each picture as a vaulting point for the next slew of facts.

"This bog body dates to 700 BC, as determined by radio-carbon dating of bone extracted from the left ankle. X-Ray fluorescence testing of the torc around her neck confirmed this as the date when the metal was forged. Her time of death was definitely during the winter, as suggested by the testing completed on hair follicles and stomach contents and by the preservation of her body.

The nitrogen levels in her finger nails were high, suggesting a higher-protein diet indicative of a Celt's winter food. This is in keeping with the food content extracted from her stomach.

"Also, because the body is so well preserved, I would imagine that the bog froze shortly after she was buried in it."

The next few photographs showed the coins taken from Mona's stomach. This was when Sean began to deliver his part of the presentation. Here he said that the body was different from other bog bodies found in the past because it was not in keeping with a ritualistic killing. The usual face-up, garroted throat, and hands tied behind the back, along with dismembered, disemboweled bodies, were all aspects of previous findings on Iron Age bog bodies and burials.

Mona was upside down and, pregnant, and a golden orb, normally used as a hair ornament, was forced into the back of her throat and then the oral cavity stuffed with peat. Her legs were whipped, and a sally rod was forced through the knees and ankles to suspend her as she was hung upside down in the boghole.

The three Roman coins in her stomach were a perplexing find. Sean had to admit that he did not know whether she was smuggling them or forced to swallow them. But the x-ray fluorescence testing of the coins revealed that they too were forged in 700 BC.
One of the board members interrupted Sean's speech about the Roman coins.

"What about the Loughshinny findings? Would that tie in with the coins found in her stomach?"

A second board member, who was also a retired forensic archaeologist, added, with an air of regret, "Unfortunately, that find is still tied up in court. We are unable to examine the discoveries at Loughshinny until all issues have been resolved legally."

Maire and Liam looked at each other and then back at the board member who last spoke. They had never heard of this find at Loughshinny.

"I am lost," Maire said, looking at Sean and then back at the group sitting around the table.

"Me too," Sean answered. His arms fell limp by his side and then shot up in the air. "What exactly was found at Loughshinny?"

"Coins and other Roman artifacts that would suggest a Roman fort once existed there," he answered, and then bit his bottom lip, for he knew what the next question was going to be.

"Where are those findings now?" asked Maire.

"Here," came the response, in a resolute and confounded tone. He knew it sounded stupid. The answer to why there were three Roman coins in Mona's stomach was at the national museum itself, but they were lawfully unable to retrieve the answer. It sounded ridiculous, even to him.

"I know, I know," he nodded. "I did not write the laws. I just try to abide by them."

"May I ask why we can't examine them?" Maire asked, almost dumbfounded at this news.

"The farmer whose land they were found on is claiming ownership. He is suing for trespassing and theft of property and has stalled the whole process for the last seventeen years. Well, technically, *he* hasn't. He died five years ago and now his son has taken up the torch, so to speak."

"But the state has rights of ownership to historical artifacts," Sean added, incredulous that they were so close to an answer, and yet, miles away from the conclusion.

"Golden coins…, money, money, money." The other board members shook their heads in agreement.

"Filthy lucre," one board member offered as a closing comment.

"How long ago were these Roman artifacts found at Loughshinny?" Sean blurted out, as if he no longer had control over anything that came out of his mouth. The words just tumbled out, effortlessly.

“The find occurred in 1987.”

“What?” Maire stuttered, narrowing her gaze and bowing her head slightly. Leaning both hands on the mahogany table, she tried to shake off the utter disbelief that she had never heard of this find, despite the fact that seventeen years had passed since 1987.

“That can’t be,” she giggled incredulously. “There has to be a mistake.”

“There is no mistake. The year was 1987 and I was present at Loughshinny when the find was removed from the site and taken to the museum.”

“Have you seen the Roman artifacts? Where are they?” Sean asked quickly, and added, “Maybe the coins in the find will match the ones we found in Mona’s stomach.”

“Who is Mona?” one of the other board members interrupted, confused and disillusioned that he had lost track of the conversation.

“We called the bog body Mona,” Sean answered.

The board member was still unclear as to why the bog body was named Mona, but a soft "Ohhh!" drifted across the table.

"Bord na Mona," Sean offered as an explanation. The board member still looked dazed.
"The Irish Turf Board." Sean volunteered this final bit of information and then decided to give up. "Not important. We'll move on."

"Do you think we might be able to match up the coins?" Sean continued.

"The case remains controversial and unresolved. The find is detained here in the museum vault, but we are not allowed to touch it until the court case is over." The senior board member knew he was sounding totally ridiculous now, but he threw his hands up to either side of his shoulders and shrugged. "I can't tell you anymore."

"Where are they…, in the vault, I mean? Whereabouts?" Maire pressed on, unwilling to accept that they were possibly standing four floors above a resolution to the most perplexing part of Mona's story.

"They are hidden." This was a new voice. It came from behind Maire and Sean. The curator of museum antiquities,

Mr. Martin, had entered the room silently and stood in a darkened corner, listening carefully to the discussion.

“Hidden?” Maire responded, nodded, and then repeated, “Hidden?” Her tone, a crescendo of disbelief, drew Martin’s deadpan; ‘I’ll have none of that now, if you please!’ looks. He eyeballed her above the rim of his glasses.

“Yes, hidden.” Mr. Martin responded.
“The most important find of the last two decades, which could prove once and for all that the Romans did make their way to Ireland, and we can’t touch the evidence because a cranky old bastard of a farmer has tied the whole lot up in court, because he thinks he should have a share of the gold?”

She leaned her entire body weight onto her two arms and pressed her hands hard into the surface of the table. Her head fell forward and she laughed an awkward, disbelieving little laugh.

Sean looked wide-eyed around the room, waiting for someone to come up with a solution to the stupidest thing he had ever heard. No one did.

“So that’s it?” he said, breaking the silence. “She makes her way out of a bog after nearly two and a half thousand years and in all of our progress and forging ahead in science we are brought to a halt because of a court case that is 17 years old?"

"Yes," said the curator and the board member who had spoken in depth about the find at Loughshinny. The others shook their heads, and finally someone said, "Continue on with your presentation of your findings."

"I think we are done," Maire said, glancing over at Sean.

"I am in a state of shock, to be honest with you," he said, "I think we could do with a bit of a break, and we will resume in an hour, is that okay?"

The five board members and the curator nodded. They would still need to discuss how Mona should be displayed and what information should be revealed to the public.

"We shall regroup in one hour," the senior board member said.

The room slowly emptied out, leaving only Maire and Liam. They immediately retrieved the photo of the coins found in Mona's stomach.

"Now I wonder what the punishment would be for going through artifacts on museum property that were tied up in litigation proceedings?" Sean said, eyeing Maire.

"Have you ever seen the vault?" Maire asked him, unable to hide her disappointment.

"No, have you?"
"Yes, it is like Fort Knox. Even if you did get past the security system, there is so much stuff down there Sean that it would take you a lifetime to go through it all."
"This only proves that she left and came back. That's all," Maire offered as an afterthought, -"If she got those coins at Loughshinny, then she was a Celt who was brought there. So why did we find her at Boteen's bog in Tipperary?"

"She was brought back to her birthplace, maybe." Maire's eyes searched for an answer in Sean's face.

"-Reluctantly by the looks of things," Sean concluded.

"Let's go back to the place where we found her. Let's take a look at some old maps and see what they tell us."

Maire bit her bottom lip and stared at the 3D computer image of Mona, now turning at a 360-degree angle on the projection screen.

She folded her arms on the table in front of her and laid her head down. “Science just raises more questions than it answers.”

“Well, in my own humble opinion,” Sean answered, “People in general are arse-holes.”
“Agreed,” Maire quipped, and sat upright.

“Let’s ask for information on the Loughshinny find and see if we can piece the puzzle together from there.”

Chapter 9

All three types of dried flower that decorated the table, the fox glove, the poppy, and the clematis, were toxic or poisonous in one way or another.
Élan smiled as she explained to Colm, while they ate, that clematis was used to induce eye, throat, and skin irritations, and that poppies were known to cause headaches. The foxgloves, or, as Élan called them, witches' gloves were widely used among the Celtic tribes to treat skin sores and lesions.

"The great mother goddess has provided us with the answer to our question. This is how we will get the Romans to free us. We will ask the Irish Celts to induce coughs, eye sores, and skin sores by rubbing the clematis on their faces and bodies. When the Romans see that we are diseased, we will have already put some poppy milk into their wine to cause headaches. We can tell them that the first sign of the disease carried by the Celts is headache. Then," she raised a dried purple foxglove, "we will ease the eye sores and skin sores of the Irish Celts when they are free, with the witches' glove!"

Colm stared, his eyes wide with disbelief.

“How do you know all this?’ he asked.

“I am my mother’s daughter,” she replied. “Although she died when I was born our house was filled with medicinal herbs and plants. Many of the women in our crannog helped me understand the use of each plant and its season of growth.”

“Will these be enough to trick the Romanii?” Colm inquired.

“No. These are not in season. It is in spring and early summer that we will find all of these plants. Bealtaine (May) is when our summer growth is in bloom. We are now at the end of Feabhra (February), so that will mean we need,” she counted on her fingers, “three full moon cycles before this can be done.”

“I have to return to Belgae before then, Élan. I must set sail with the Celts of my tribe before Bealtaine.”
“Then do what you must do. But do not take members of my tribe as slaves,” her warning strong and unwavering.

“How can I not take them?” Colm asked, pondering how this could come to be.

“Let us see…?” Élan said, as she took the white spray of clematis and rubbed it into her left arm. Within moments, the skin was red and a rash began to spread. “Now, for the remedy,” she said, rubbing the fox glove vigorously onto her forearm. They both watched as the rash slowly subsided.

"Eat with me each day. I will make sure that these flowers decorate our table, and we will save them for your tribe. It will be enough to induce sickness so as to keep you all quarantined from the Romans until my return at the end of Bealtaine."

Colm was alive with hope. "By the time I arrive, I will have spread word that Celts in Europa have been hit with disease. I will be a potential carrier of this disease. By the time I arrive, the fields will be overflowing with fresh plants like these."

"When will you leave?" she asked, holding his hand in hers.

"In a fort night," he responded, tilting nearer to her.

"Lie with me tonight?" he asked, leaning closer still, to kiss her.

"No," she responded, after she had kissed him. "You will lie with me, for it is I who choose you as my first husband. The choice is mine, not yours, Colm. I take you freely and give myself freely as your wife."
"You took my people and land away from me," she said, as she stroked his hair and they both leaned back into the bed of straw.

"I know, and I regret my actions on that day. How can I make amends with you? I cannot bring the dead back to life."

He was above her now and he kissed her face and her hair.

"Take us back to the crannog, and have a life with me there. Let me be free like my mother was. I will take you freely as my husband and we will have children together."

"What about Liam Ruadh?" he asked, "He will surely kill us both."

"He is of the new ways; he treats me like a servant. I want a man who will treat me as his equal. Neither of us can exist without the other, Colm. Male cannot be here without female. Female cannot exist without male. We coexist peacefully, are equally as important, and need each other to live. Liam Ruadh will remain here; let the great mother goddess deal with him in our absence. Nature will take her course with Liam Ruadh."

"I understand," he said, as he kissed her on the lips. When he raised his face, she took his hand, and it now made its way, with her hand guiding it, beneath her robes and across her cool, vibrant flesh, and felt the pointed nipple of her breast. He felt himself stiffen, and knowing that she wanted him as one with her, he pressed himself harder into her. "Yes," she said

longingly. "We will lie together tonight and tomorrow night and each night until you leave, and then when you return we will lie together every night until we are done with each other."
His lips again found hers, and the hunger within him for every part of her body was unbearable. When he entered, he moved in and out gently, and when he had finished, he kissed her face and they lay together, silently, listening to each other's breathing, hearing the winds of February creeping, like a wild animal, around the stone dwelling.

"I will set sail in the middle of Marta (March); the seas will be a little calmer then. A fortnight. We have a fortnight to set the plan into action," Colm said, thinking aloud.

"I must return to my tribesmen and-women to inform them of the plan. By Bealtaine, the flowers will be growing wildly and abundantly on the hills. Mind now to use the red flower, the poppy for your purpose," she said, as she stirred beside him.

She arose and pulled the Romanii robes of white over her naked body. He held his hand out to caress the last piece of naked flesh before it disappeared beneath white robes. She draped the robes around her for more warmth. Then she took the dried flowers and wrapped them in a fold at the front.

"Walk with me?" she asked, as she pulled his hand, which was draped over the edge of the bed. He stood, dressed, and pulled her into him again for a final kiss before leaving the stone dwelling.

"I am reborn," he said, as he released her.
"I have given birth to new life within you." Élan replied as she stroked the side of his face with the smoothness of the back of her hand, allowing her fingers to glide gently across his lips.

"I cannot exist without you," Colm said.

"Nor I you," she said. "It is as it should be."

He walked her back to the stone house where the Irish Celts were held captive, and she returned to her original spot among the men who earlier had talked of plans to escape. Neither she nor Colm acted as a lover would in front of the Irish Celts. They were not ready for that news. Liam Ruadh was the first to speak when Colm left them.

"What did he do with you?" He barked at her, unable to disguise his jealousy.
"Nothing," she lied. "We ate in silence. Have you all eaten?"

Murmurs of yes spread throughout the small group.

“Did they use flowers to decorate the table?” she inquired.

“What table?” someone added, “They brought us a cooked pheasant and bread and water. We had no table Élan.”

“They fed us the same, but the table was decorated with dried flowers…; witches’ gloves, clematis, and red poppies.”

“Thank you for sharing your glorious evening with us, Élan. Perhaps now we can get back to planning an escape,” Liam Ruadh said, in a staccato and biting tone.

“I was talking about our escape, Liam. Please do not interrupt me again,” she added, and watched him leap over the Celts seated in front of him, his hand raised and threatening to strike her.

The closest Celt grabbed Liam’s hand in midair and bent his arm back forcing him to fall to his knees. “Let her speak,” came the voice of the younger Celt.

“The flowers induce eye, skin, and throat irritations, as well as headache. And then the fox glove is the remedy.” She sat on the straw amidst the tribe. This was her rightful place, and the others knew it. She was a natural, unbiased, and fair leader.

"What is the plan for these poisonous flowers, Élan?" Grainne's voice came, low and husky, from the dark gray shadows.

"I will dine with the Fir Bolg warrior each night for the next two weeks. I will return here with dried clematis each night, and when the Fir Bolg tribe returns to Belgae, we will induce skin, eye, and throat irritations to cause the Romans to be concerned; concerned enough to quarantine us. They will not know whether it is simply a weather sickness or a deadly disease. After six weeks, the Fir Bolg tribe will return from Europa with the story that a deadly disease is sweeping through the Celtic tribes of Europa and Ireland. We will also have used poppies, for they will be in season by Bealtaine, to poison the wine and cause the Romanii to have headaches, which we will tell them is the first sign of the disease."

"They will release us as diseased and dying Celts," Grainne said in astonishment. "We will pick the fox-gloves on our way back to the crannog to relieve our irritations."

"Yes!" Élan was delighted that the only other person in the tribe to get her plan instantly was another female.

"That is the mind of a true leader at work!" exclaimed the younger Celt.

"Why should the Fir Bolg warrior want to help us?" Liam asked, knowing what the response was going to be, but just waiting to attack when it came.

"Because he laments what has happened. My father was a good man, and they knew each other in younger days." She could hold the truth in no longer. "You killed my father, Liam, not Colm Riordán, although I am still trying to understand why."

Liam made a violent, mad move toward Élan, but a foot caught him in the temple, and he fell backward in darkness. The young Celt and Liam wrestled to overpower one another. The older Liam was no match for the young, wily Celt. He grasped Liam's hands behind his back and pushed him face-down into the straw.

"You were to be the next chieftain," Grainne again responded. "That is why Liam reacted violently."

Grainne had been the chieftain's fourth wife, and his only aide in sickness. She stood up and addressed the group.

"My husband, our last chieftain, had middle-of-the-night meetings in his hut with Diarmuid. Diarmuid confessed to him that Liam had spied on himself and Élan going on moonlit hunts. When Diarmuid told the chieftain of the bargain Liam Ruadh had negotiated on that night, in return for his silence and an agreement for no more hunting, the chieftain's concerns were confirmed. Liam Ruadh is a corrupt and tainted man."

"What bargain?" asked the young Celt, restraining Liam's hands with rags.

"Liam was forcing Diarmuid to give him Élan as his wife." Grainne said.

"He is not a leader. He negotiated for his own benefit," the Celt said, and rounding his fist into a tight ball, he plunged it into Liam's right jaw and, left him unconscious on the floor.
"In shock that an Irish Celt would barter his silence in exchange for a Celtic woman, not allowing her to choose freely, the chieftain was disillusioned. It was upon hearing Liam's terms of negotiation, on that night with Diarmuid, that the chieftain decided that, both he and Diarmuid, would secretly train Élan to be the next chieftain of the tribe. Unknown to you, Élan, the talks of war tactics, lessons in leadership, and discourses on fairness, and the sense of community amongst the tribe were all gearing you for your future role as our tribal chieftain." Grainne faced Élan, smiling. "My husband picked a good leader as our next Chieftain."
Élan stood and hugged Grainne.

“I never knew why we had endless discussions on how to deal with tribal issues, but now I understand,” Élan said.

“I myself wondered until this very instant whether he made the right decision. Each time he met with your father, he would discuss the next lesson in your leadership. You will be a fair, consistent, and wise chieftain, Élan.” Grainne nodded her approval and then added, “When do we start?”

By the time Liam Ruadh came to, his feet and hands had been bound with rags. He struggled and gave up instantly.

Élan was no more than two steps from his face when she asked, “Why did you kill him?”

“Because he was going to create a new way of life, with the Fir Bolg’s assistance, and my role of chieftain would never come to be,” Liam answered, filled with poison.

“It wasn’t going to happen anyway, Liam.” The young Celt’s voice came from the darkness, beside Liam. “The chieftain had already abandoned all hope of ever educating you to be a fair, consistent, and good leader. He was educating Élan for that role.”

"I was the one!" Liam yelled. "Not her…, I am the chieftain now! Not a stupid woman who just gives birth. She is mindless in her talk of flowers and poisons. What does any woman know of leadership and war and death? Men are the leaders! We are the leaders! The men shall lead, not the women!"

"Bind his mouth closed," said Grainne. She tore another piece of rag from the hem of her tunic. "I can't listen to him anymore."

"So he did kill Diarmuid, just as Colm said," the young Celt added, as he bound Liam's mouth with the rag.

"Yes. He killed a fellow tribesman, and now he thinks he still qualifies as a tribal chieftain." Élan looked at him. She shook her head and said, "You will be gagged all day and left in the shadows. Only for food will we remove the mouth gag. When it is time for us to leave this place, you will not come with us. You are no longer of our tribe, Liam. We will not kill you. My way is to spare life if possible. We will spare your life, and then, of course, it is up to the Romanii to decide your fate, after we are cast out with our sickening plague."

Two Celts dragged Liam back into the shadows.

"We'll sleep now and begin the storing of the clematis tomorrow."

"Here, Élan, this stone is ill placed, and there is a space behind it. We will store the clematis there until it is time to use it." Grainne stood in the back of the stone house and held a large stone away from the wall, revealing a chamber of sorts behind.

"Is he bound and gagged well?" Élan asked.

The younger Celt checked all of Liam's bindings. "He won't break free of those with any great speed," he said.

"Let us sleep for now and begin anew tomorrow," she said.

Élan found her spot close to the door and nestled herself into the straw. Her eyes closed, and she saw Colm before her. She remembered his gracefulness and soft nature with her and longed to be with him again. Soon she was sleeping soundly.

The next morning Colm explained to the Roman leader that he would be leaving in two weeks. The change of season would have passed by then, and the winds would have died down, making the waters calmer. He would not bring any slaves with him, as they seemed weak, and he would rather have them make the journey in better health. "No money in dead Celts, only in

live ones," he told the Roam leader. The Romanii agreed to keep the Celts fed and watered in exchange for stronger slaves and the finely decorated wine flagons of La Tène, and some cauldrons with decoration also.
So it was agreed; gifts plundered from other Celts in Europe in exchange for keeping the Irish slaves alive.

Each night Élan dined with Colm and returned to the Celtic captives with the white poisonous flower called clematis held beneath her Roman robe. Grainne hid the flowers behind the rock, and within ten nights, there was enough to last for the entire time that Colm would be away. His time away would total six weeks. He asked that Élan be served food in his stone house each night while he was gone. The six weeks passed quickly, and Colm began his journey back to mainland Europe.

Colm bartered enameled brooches, and cape pins taken from Ireland; the Irish Celts were the only ones who had mastered this art of enameling. In return he received wine flagons, torcs, golden decorative hair orbs, and other Celtic pieces, as he traveled throughout Europe. Some items he would part with to the Romanii back at the fort in Ireland. Other pieces he would gift quietly to Élan, upon his return.
Each night she retrieved the clematis and returned to the Celts with their flowers to freedom. It was agreed amongst them all that the irritation should commence two weeks after Colm had

left. It would be painful, but it was their only hope. Liam Ruadh remained gagged except to eat. He would not be part of this plan, and he would not be coming with them, either.
It was also agreed between Colm and Élan that he should return with a flagon of mead for the Roman Leader. The mead would be tainted with poppy milk, for upon Colm's return, the poppies would be in full bloom. Élan explained carefully how he would gently put pressure on the stems of the poppies and release the juice into the flagon of mead. The Roman leader and his guests would feel the effects of the poppy milk after a day or two; they would be unlikely to make the link between their headaches and the tainted mead. It was more likely that they would connect them with the eye sores, skin sores, and barking coughs of the Celtic prisoners, who would seem diseased beyond use by the time Colm arrived back to Ireland.

The last night between Colm and Élan passed beautifully. He was hers, and she his. Her heart was low when he left, but he promised to return and lead her to safety and a new life with him back at the crannog. The Romans understood that she was his woman and left her alone, except to feed her each night in his stone dwelling.

Four weeks after Colm left, the clematis had taken its full effect on the Irish Celts. Red skin, scalded and sore eyes, and bad coughs afflicted all, making the Romans keep their distance.

Élan seemed sicklier than the others. So sick that the Romans no longer walked her to and from Colm's stone dwelling, but instead brought the food to her with the other Celts.

The smell of meat made her stomach sick, and often she would retch so much that her stomach contents would not remain inside her. Dry bread was the only thing she managed to keep down.

One evening, as the sun of late April loomed huge and orange in the sky before setting; Grainne sat beside her and held her hand. Both women had red-rimmed eyes and sores on their mouths now, from five weeks of rubbing the clematis on their faces and arms. The stone dwelling was filled with coughing and groans. The Romans left the food at the threshold of the door, no longer willing to go inside. They really did not know if this was the effects of ill weather and no warmth inside the stone dwelling, or if it was something more serious. Advised by the leader, they did not touch any Celt, or help them in any way.

As the other Celts pulled meat from the leg of the animal being devoured, Grainne took some bread and tore it in two, giving Élan half and keeping the other for herself.

"You are with child," she said quietly, so as not to let the others hear.

"I am?" Élan asked in disbelief.

"Have you bled in the last six weeks?"

Élan thought and then responded, "No."

"Then you are with child," Grainne said.

Élan sat quietly and stared at the orange blaze in the April skyline above the fortress wall. How could she tell Grainne that Colm was the father of her child? He was not of their tribe, he had taken them from their crannog and brought them here as slaves.

"He is a good man," Grainne volunteered as if she was reading Élan's thoughts.

"What?" Élan whispered, tears coming to her eyes.

"What does it matter that he is Fir Bolg or from Belgae; we are all Celts, are we not? We are more alike than we are different. He was raised a warrior, and you have changed him. He is making amends for what he has done. That is what matters. Now eat your bread, you will need to feed two people."

"Thank you, Grainne," Élan whispered, as she slowly ate the grainy bread and watched the sun set. She wished for Colm to return.

"Two more weeks…, a fortnight," Grainne added, "and we will be free and on our way home."

By the time Colm had made his way back, he had hidden clothes and jewelry from Celtic tribes in Europe in a large tree with a hole in its center in a field in the distance, behind the fort. These would be Élan's gifts; clothing, jewelry, and resins from far-off Europe. He found his way back to the fortress, telling his fellow tribesmen not to enter with him. Word had spread, he said, of a disease outbreak amongst the Romans and the Celts in the Fortress.

"Wait for me on the shores of Loughshinny," he said. "I will return if things do not look well. If I do not return in two days, set sail, and protect yourselves."

When his own tribe had retreated to the shoreline, Colm headed toward the promontory fort.

On the hillside, the red poppies dotted the green grass in abundance, just as Élan had predicted. Colm squeezed twenty poppies each into the two flagons of mead and then went on to the Roman Fort.

He nodded at the Roman soldiers, and went first to his stone dwelling to drop off his bartering loot, and then to the Celts' stone house. Élan lay in a heap at the door, coughing and covered with sores on her flesh. Colm went to her, but she motioned for him not to touch her. He was close enough to hear her whisper.

Panicked at how badly she looked, he asked, "Is it supposed to be this bad?"

Nodding slowly, she added, "Colm, I am also with child, your child."

He moved forward to hug her. Again she shook her head, "They need to believe that this is contagious, and bad."

"You are with child?" he whispered softly, and again she nodded.

Now they would *have* to make their way to freedom and make their new lives together.

"I will be fine once we get to use the fox-gloves," she said. "Now go and tell the Romanii we have an incurable and contagious disease. Make them believe we have a plague. Make them release us as soon as possible."

Colm grabbed his bag which was filled with both flagons of mead and some decorative cups, decorative cloaks, and a small cauldron. He returned to the Roman soldiers guarding the gate, asking them who guarded the entrance way to the courtyard and how long the Celts had been sick. They told him the Irish Celts had been truly sick like this for four to five weeks now. He poured them each a cup of mead.

"If they continue to get worse, it is not good. The Celtic fringe of Europa has lost almost half of its tribes due to a strange illness that causes death."

The Roman soldiers shook their heads, asked how bad it was, and was it easy to get the disease. He assured them that human-to-human contact was the only way to get the disease, or so he was told. They drank more mead. "This is good," one said, and the other nodded.

"You haven't touched any of them, have you?" Colm asked, watching them finish off the last of the cool, tainted mead.

"We deliver a leg of meat and remove the bone at the break of dawn."

"But the disease could be on the bone!" Colm added, shaking his head. Both soldiers looked at each other now, worried that they had come in contact with a deadly disease.

"The first symptom is headache. Let me know if you feel ill in anyway. I'll talk to your leader and request that these Celts be driven from this fortress so as not to spread the disease further amongst the Romanii."

The Roman leader delighted in his new gifts, ornate and beautiful as they were. The flagons of mead were so intricate with their fashioned bronze resting deer and handles that looked like a branch of a tree with small buds growing from it.

The cloak Colm gifted to the Roman leader's wife was of a deep red fabric with an ornate gold trim depicting half-human half, and half-animal beings in strong defensive poses. The Roman leader said he was aware that the Celts held captive were sick, but the soldiers had not been near or seen any of them in daylight, so he believed the Romanii were safe. He continued to talk as he enjoyed two and then three cups of the sweet, honey mead and, then, offered some to his wife and other guests at his table.

Boasting of how one day all Celts would be in service to the Romanii and how this damp and dreary island of Ireland would serve Rome well as a penal colony, he continued on and on and slighted Colm's remarks that a disease was hitting the Celtic fringes of Europe hard, wiping out great numbers.

"Your soldiers," Colm added, "have been handling bones that the Celts have eaten from. I have told them to warn us of changes in their health as soon as possible."

"What are the symptoms of this Celtic disease?" the Roman leader's wife asked, as she emptied her newly acquired, highly decorated La Tène goblet of the honey mead.

"Head-ache is the first sign, but not a sure sign of certain death. Those who removed themselves from those who were afflicted seem to have beaten death."

"Should we be concerned for our own health?" she added, with great amounts of dramatic flair.

"Only if you suspect you are suffering a symptom," Colm reassured her.

When the evening came to an end, Colm assured the Roman leader that both flagons were from La Tène and designed to keep the wine or mead cool. They were easily cleaned by unscrewing the base, which was easily screwed back on after the flagon was cleaned. These were indeed highly desired and valuable pieces of Celtic art-work for the Romanii.

“We shall make a decision in the morning about whether or not to drive out the diseased Celts.”

“A wise decision, I agree,” Colm added, and then went back to his dwelling.

He did not sleep that night. He too had kept some clematis hidden beneath a stone in the wall, and he rubbed it into his face, on to the flesh of his arms, and all over his neck. By dawn, his flesh was alive with itch, so badly that he wanted to rip his skin, and his eyes were rimmed red and bloodshot.

The Roman Leader was already making his way across the cobblestone courtyard to Colm’s dwelling and was met by the two Romans who were guarding the Celts the night before. They held their heads as if they were unable to support the weight of their own skulls.

“What are you doing? Why are you not guarding the Celtic prisoners?”- he barked.

“The first symptom.., our heads ache!” one blurted out, almost in tears.

“Send two more in your place,” the Roman Leader ordered.

Colm emerged from his dwelling into the daylight when he heard the Roman leader call,-“Riordán! I need to speak with you.”

The Roman leader took one look at Colm and stepped backwards, almost stumbling in shock at what he saw.

“You and the other Celts must leave…, -leave now. Take them all with you. You are diseased, and we will not be safe with you here.”

Colm nodded in agreement. His eyes, face, neck, upper arms, and hands were covered in blotches.

“You will be fine so long as you remain clear of diseased people. I will get the others, and we will go and die away from here, in the woods of the interior of Ireland. Thank you for your kindness to me. You will be fine once we all leave. If other Fir Bolgs come, send them away. Tell them I was diseased and was sent off to die.”

Both men nodded at each other, and the Roman leader shook his head. “Now I just want to return to Rome. The emperor will have to forget this ridiculous idea of a penal colony. This island is cursed, diseased!” he said, holding an end of his immaculate, white tunic to his mouth.
“I know, friend, I know,” Colm replied.

The Roman Leader felt the first pang of pain in his right temple, his hand shot up in self-defense mode to massage it, and then the pain hit hard. By the time he had returned to his dwelling, his wife and all the guests that had dined with them the night before were all afflicted with head pain.
“Set them adrift in this wilderness and desolate place they call Ireland!” his wife yelled, and then held her head in protection against the shrillness of her own voice.

One of the guests had such a bad reaction to the mead and poppy mixture that he soiled himself, adding to the illusion that they had come desperately close to a plagued people.

Upon seeing a man soil himself, and watching brown, watery liquid seeping through the white robes at his legs, a woman began to vomit, and again the effect and illusion were astounding. The plague was closing in on the Romanii.

"Release the Celts and drive them out of the fortress," the Roman leader yelled to centurions below his window in the courtyard. The flagons, goblets, and cloak, all the great gifts of the day before were discarded into a stone pit. Fearful that they carried the disease, the Romans kept nothing of Colm's gifts.

The Romans watched from a safe distance, amidst soiling themselves and heaving their stomachs dry, as the Celts struggled, stumbling toward the entrance way to the fortress, now their gateway to freedom.

Outside the gates, fox-gloves bloomed in abundance in their beautiful colors, and the Celts smiled at each other and coughed and laughed as they picked flowers and rubbed them on their bodies. Some even sucked the juice from the stems. They walked slowly for about two hours and then rested in a field. Colm showed his hiding place for his hoard of La Tène jewelry and clothing to his wife, Élan.

From a large, burlap-type sack inside the hollow of the tree, Colm produced a beautiful neck torc. On either end was a deer's head. The metal was twisted into spirals, and he reminded her that the leaves and flowers and deer heads were what made La Tène famous among Celtic blacksmiths. He placed it around her neck. It was solid gold and felt heavy to her.

Colm then showed her the most ornate and decorated piece of clothing Élan had ever seen. It was a tunic of deep red with bands of gold on the sleeves and hemline and square neckline. Half- human, half-animal like beings in mighty poses were all engrained into the gold-band trim. She touched the material; it was so soft, she couldn't believe it was clothing to be worn on her own body. It was fur lined with leather. The deep red color was achieved through the art of dying, which the Celts in Europe had mastered.

She quickly stripped off the filthy Roman tunic, which was was no longer splendidly white, and it was then that he saw her tiny, bulging belly. He placed his hand on her stomach, and he bent to kiss it. He knelt on the ground and kissed her stomach again and then enveloped her in his arms. She placed her hands on his head coughed a little, and stroked his hair. He stood up right and kissed her lips, and then helped her put on her new red tunic. She looked beautiful in it. Her skin glowed in the deep hue of the red.

"We will keep the white tunic in case the fur of this new dress irritates your skin," he said, and kissed her forehead again. "We will rest here, Élan."

Colm assured her as they returned to the rest of the tribe, now sitting in the shade of vivid new green leaves and long grass, as the white, clean- sunshine of early May shafted its way through the leaves, that more fox gloves grew all around, and relief was not far away.

"Already my cough has eased," she said, as he helped her find a comfortable place to sit. Colm had also managed to take bread with him; he passed it out among the Celts, and they thanked him for it. He then picked more fox gloves and passed those around, too.

"How long before the fox-gloves take effect and the ill effects of the clematis are gone?" Colm asked Élan.

She answered, "In two or three days we will no longer cough, and our sores will have started to heal."

"By then the Romans will no longer feel the effects of the poppy juice, but they will have no idea where to begin looking for us," Colm replied, and they both nodded and smiled. The plan had worked, and they were free.

"It was a good plan," Colm said.

"It was a great plan, but a painful one," Grainne chimed in suddenly, and some of the other Celts laughed in agreement.

"What of Liam Ruadh?" Colm inquired. "You left him there?"

"Yes, he is no longer a tribesman. He is deceitful and dishonest, and he dislikes women as leaders," Grainne added.

"Yet I killed your chieftain, and I am still permitted in your midst." Colm was not sure of his own safety now. Élan sensed his unease and gripped his hand slightly and then tightly wrapped her fingers around it.

The younger Celtic male who had sided with Élan all through the captivity ordeal spoke up.

"Our chieftain was a wise man, Colm. But he was an old and very sick man. Grainne has told us of his secret meetings with Élan's father and his desire for Élan, not Liam, to be chieftain of our tribe. Yes, you caused us to leave our crannog and killed our chieftain, but he was dying. Had it not been for this forced captivity, we would probably still be living at the crannog, under the corrupt leadership of Liam Ruadh. The tribe would have been divided under his leadership, and our women would have had no say in their own lives. He told us that women were nothing, that men came first."

"He believed that the new ways of the Warrior Cult are better than the old," Colm added, "but I suppose I am living proof that the older ways of worship, those of the mother goddess, are fair to both women and men and are more peaceful. I was educated as a warrior, and I have taken many lives, but it is this life beside me now that brings me the only true joy I have ever known, because she chose me." He kissed Élan's hand and then asked forgiveness of the crowd of Celtic men and women around him.

"Forgive me if you can find it in your hearts, for the lives I have taken from your crannog. Let me be of service to you now in whatever way I can until the day I die."

"Take good care of our new chieftain. That is all we ask of you, Colm, and never lift a sword again." The young Celt laughed as he spoke, and Colm thanked him, reassuring him that his days of killing were over. He looked at Élan and said, "On my love for you, Élan, I swear never to take another life from this land."

***

Liam Ruadh lay huddled in the darkness of the stone dwelling. He had been tied to a wooden beam that lay near the back wall. It was such a large beam that he could not move it. But after three days of slight rubbing, the rag had frayed so much that it was with little to no effort that he pulled his wrists apart and began to untie the gaga from his mouth and then the rags from his legs.

He stumbled into the bright sunshine of May. The Celts were now three days on the move and were only one quarter of the way back to the crannog. The entire fort had been left deserted. The Romanii had fled so as not to get the terrible Celtic disease. The leader, however, had remembered to pack the second flagon of mead, the only gift he had not discarded, and continued to enjoy this new drink when the ill effects of the head ache had finally disappeared after three days.

Liam wandered the fort in search of food, bread, and water, but little was found. One soldier remained, for he had a true sickness and was believed to be dying of the Celtic disease, so he too was left abandoned.

Afraid that this Celt would kill him and devour him, as his leaders had led him to believe, the soldier reached into his money bag, threw a handful of gold coins at Liam, and shouted. “Andare via Keltoi! Go away, Celt!”

Liam gathered the coins and counted eight. He would use these as gifts to buy the hospitality of other tribes until he reached his own crannog. He was weak, but he knew the eastern shores of Ireland better than Colm or Élan did. He made his way to Dun Laoghaire and talked his way into another Celtic tribe who fed him and restored him to health. In return, he entertained them with stories of his travels in Meath, or middle Ireland, a place they were not familiar with, and also of the Romanii, whom they were familiar with but preferred to keep clear of.

In the middle of October, Deirdhe Fomhair, Liam bid his farewell to the Celtic tribe at Dun Laoghaire and thanked them for restoring him to good health. Here he parted with two of his coins and then roamed onward to his next resting site. He told his hosts that he was determined to join his own tribe for the great celebration and feasts of Samhain, and they believed him, for the feast of Samhain was an important festival among the Irish Celts.

"Get to your tribe before the sidhes open up on Samhain's eve and release the dead to roam freely." The tribal chieftain warned Liam, as he left the long house and then the crannog.

"I *am* the freely roaming dead," Liam said, as he made his way through the forests of Meath and toward the north shore of Lough Derg.

The first frost had come and gone, and the weather was turning much colder. By the time he neared the shores of Lough Derg, he had been the beneficiary of three other tribes' hospitality, and almost six months had passed. When the terrain became more familiar to him, he had been walking for seven months and had lived among many tribes. He had four Roman coins remaining.

The bulrushes to his right reminded him that the Shannon was near, and the crannog was not too far away, either. Samhain would be his night to return; it was a good night to encounter those he needed to do business with, because it was the night of the dead.

***

Élan was now eight moon cycles with child, and she was ready for her child to enter the world. Colm had told her that the new fashion in Europe among the males and females was to lighten their hair with limestone and, then fashion it into braids with a resin from Spain and place golden orbs at the ends of the braids. The shorter the male, the higher his hair was piled on his head and set in place, like a large knot, with this plant resin.

“It makes short men seem tall, see?” he laughed.

“What about making tall men look short?” she said, rubbing the back of his neck as he sat and ate.

“Or how about making a tall woman even taller,” he shot back, and she pinched him.

He rubbed his hand over her belly, and she felt the warm fur inside the tunic brush up against her bare skin. There was a quick kick from the baby, and Colm's smile stretched wide. "I felt that! Did you feel that too?"

"I felt nothing!" she said, poking him in the stomach. "The baby is growing inside me! I feel every move!"

Seven months had passed, and their crannog was regaining its life. Other tribal members had come to them for shelter, they too the victims of Fir Bolg attacks. No Fir Bolg had attacked since the Romanii had begun to spread the tale of the horrendous and deadly Irish Celtic disease. Even Colm's own Fir Bolg warriors had deserted him, believing he was a victim of the disease.

Liam Ruadh was believed to be dead, starved to death and rotting away in the stone dwelling at the Roman fort. They never mentioned him anymore.

"Samhain is upon us soon. My mother chose my father on Samhain," she said distractedly. "She said he moved like a deer, quietly and gracefully. She was older than him."

"He told me she was wise," Colm added sensing a melancholy in her voice. She went to sit on the rudimentary wooden chair and leaned on the table.

"All six siblings have gone. I have no parents to share this baby with."

Her mood was low; he walked to her and sat hunkered beside her.

"I am here, a stór, I am here." It was the first time he had used the Gaelic word for darling. She snapped into the present.
"Say that again," she asked leaning her forehead against his and stroking his jawline gently with her fingers.

"I am here, a stór, I am here."

"Lime stone makes your hair lighter?" Her voice seemed brighter.

"Yes," he answered. "Shall we try it and lighten our humor and our hair?"

"Get me some limestone, a stór," she commanded endearingly.

"I have the plant resin, too," Colm said, producing an ornate vase and leaving it steadily on the table.
She took the cork out and sniffed it. "It smells good," she said, surprised.

"I think you should style your hair and decorate yourself with the golden orbs for Samhain," Colm said, trying very hard to lighten her mood, and now starting to prepare the ground lime.

They were now living in the same hut that her mother and father had lived in and where she and her father had lived. He knew that she was glad to be back in the crannog, but she was sometimes sad, reminded of how things had changed.

"I have a meeting with the Tánaiste and other tribal members after sunset," she remembered suddenly. "I love being married to the chieftain," Colm said, as he began replacing the cork on the resin vase and clearing the cups and bowls from the table.

"We will talk of our plans for Samhain and our food stocks for winter."

"How are the stocks of food?" Colm asked eagerly.

She answered, "We definitely need to increase our store. Do you feel like a bit of night hunting? It is going to be a full moon tonight."

"Only if you promise to stay here, and I will go with Eoghain," came Colm's response.

"You go on the moonlight hunts after the child has made its way into the world, and I will stay home with our first-born," he chuckled quietly, watching her pull her long wavy brunette hair back and bundle it together in an ornate enameled cloak pin he had found on the shelf; it was her mother's, an ancient gift from her husband the blacksmith.

"I will tell the Tánaiste tonight that you and he will go hunting later to increase our food store."

She went to him and, embraced his waist, as he bent forward to kiss her.

"Good-bye, Chieftain. I will look forward to your return," he said.

The Tánaiste, Eoghain, was the young Celt who had sided with her at the Roman Fort. Grainne was the senior member of the council now. Ten other tribal members, equal numbers of males and females, were in attendance. As she predicted, they spoke of their plans for Samhain and the need to replenish food stores for the winter.

When the meeting was over, she returned to her hut, and Eoghain came with her. Colm and the Tánaiste both set out across the bridge into the forest, and Élan lay down on the straw bed.

In the dying embers of the fire, she saw them sitting at either side of the doorway: Her father and her mother, just as he had described her, his voice, inside Élan's head, giving her a detailed description of the green eyes, long blonde hair, and luminescent skin.

"She was fawn like," she heard his voice remind her, "Her green eyes spoke, and she never said a word."

"I have your eyes," Élan said, and felt a tear trickle over the bridge of her nose and down her left cheek. She looked at her father. "I have your hair."

When she closed her eyes she then began to dream that her baby had been born and both her mother and her father were still alive. Each one held the baby and kissed its forehead. The child looked like Colm, Etain, Diarmuid, and herself.

When Colm returned, she awoke and cried, "I want them to be here." He knew exactly who she meant, and he held her and felt useless, and said, "I know, Élan."

They both lay back into the straw and eventually drifted off to sleep. In her dreams, again she saw both of her parents. They were waiting, silently, and smiling while they waited. Her mother held a baby in her arms. When she awoke the next morning, she told Colm of her visions. He said that women nearing childbirth might have vivid dreams, but he wasn't sure. Trying to change her mood, and remove the stress she was feeling, he began to talk of lightening their hair that day.

"This day, I declare you a fair-haired, beautiful Irish Celt," he said, as he crushed limestone into a fine powder on the floor of the hut. When he had helped her apply the limestone and water paste to her hair and then wash it away, she declared her disappointment. "This is not fair hair Colm, this is red hair."

"I know," he said smiling. "It is even more beautiful."

"Then I will keep it this way," was her declaration.

"Will you use the resin to help keep the orbs in my braids for the feast?" she asked him.

"I'll show you how they use it by styling my own hair in a Suebian knot, and then you can do your hair in this way if you choose."

"A Suebian knot will make you look like a tall, white tree, Colm." She laughed as she imagined him looking taller than he already was.

"You just want all the resin for yourself, Chieftain," he replied, smiling, happy that she had laughed.

"No, you would look too tall," she said.

"No resin for me, then," Colm said as he smeared a little on her cheek.

"Oh, it feels strange! But it smells good."

"You, my darling wife, will be the most beautiful Chieftain ever to lead the feast of Samhain."

She smiled and added, "We have united many Celts from many lands." She lifted the vase of plant resin. "The Celts of Spain." She then pointed to her tunic and said, "The La Tène Celts," and then to her newly dyed red hair. "And those fighting Fir Bolgs of Belgae," and they both laughed.
"Come here to me, beautiful Irish Celt."

Colm placed his hand on her pregnant stomach and slowly rubbed it.

"Our child," he said, looking at her belly and then at her face. "A true Celt," she said and they both smiled at her remark.

"I must away; the men are building the bonfire, so my help is needed."

"Go then," she said, slapping him on the behind, "do your men's work and leave me to my woman's work."

She watched him stoop as he made his way out of the hut. "This was a wonderful feeling," she thought to herself, "a feeling that I am where I should be."

The entrance to the hut revealed the falling darkness outside as she readied herself in her finery for the feast. Colm's beautiful gifts, the tunic and torc, seemed to make her hair look even lighter. As she placed the torc around her neck, she heard Colm return through the entrance.

Without turning to greet him, she said, "It must be a very small bonfire we are having this feast?"

A hand clamped itself heavily over her mouth.

Chapter 10

"We need to know some more information about the Loughshinny find," Maire said, as she pushed her way through Martin's office door.

"Don't you believe in knocking anymore, Maire?" Martin said dryly, as he swiveled in his chair and turned toward her and Sean.

"Listen here," she said, a tiny spray of spittle spraying on Martin's glasses, "You knew about the Roman coins because you saw the hoard from Loughshinny, not because Sean was holding the coins in a plastic bag in his hands! He had them in his pocket all along. Why would you hide information like that from us? Why would you do that?"

Sean stood in the background, gulping down his shock. He had never seen Maire act so ballsy in all the time he had worked with her. She had always been polite to other work-mates, but this was uncharacteristically nervy behavior for her.

“I withheld information, Maire, because of the next question you are going to ask, and my answer to that question will be no.”

Martin peered at her over the rim of his glasses and then, slowly, removed them, folded the side wings closed, and placed them on his desk, lost in his thoughts. He turned and folded his arms across his chest, waiting with complete certainty for the question to come.

“Let us examine the Loughshinny find, and we will not breathe a word of it to anyone.”

He shook his head and then asked, “What good would it do? I was there in 1987, I knew because of the CAT scan technician’s disk, and we both know as much as the other. The Roman coins in her stomach are the same as the ones from Loughshinny. What good does that do us now?”

“We might find some clues as to why she was murdered,” Maire added, incredulous that she even needed to explain that to him.

Sean watched in the background, his head moving from right to left as if watching a long tennis volley. He wasn’t quite sure yet who was in the lead, but the volley was going fairly well.

"But, sure, I can give you that information myself," Martin said, and then added, "However, you will not be able to use it in your presentation, as it alludes to the fact that you've examined the Loughshinny hoard, which, as I have previously mentioned, we are unable to do as dictated to us by law."
"It is a stupid law!" Maire said, exasperated by the technicality of the entire Loughshinny legalities.
"Yes, it is," Martin replied, "and there is nothing we can do about it. Take a seat there again." He motioned to the two seats they had sat on the day before.

"Maire, I have been chomping at the bit for the last seventeen years for this Loughshinny issue to be resolved! Don't you think that I would love to go through the find and prove that there was a Roman Coastal Fort at Dromanagh near Loughshinny? Think of what a change that would be to Irish history as we know it!"

Maire and Sean sat in the creaky chairs, and Martin leaned forward to emphasize what he was saying.

"Sure, the history books would have to be rewritten all over the world. The Roman Empire extended to Ireland! What a great reveal for all those involved in the find!"

"Have you seen some of the artifacts?" Sean asked, not knowing if he was ready to believe the answer, since Martin had lied so well on the previous day.

"Yes, as I have said, that is why I knew that you had found Roman coins in her stomach."

"You saw Roman coins just like the ones we found?" Maire asked.

"Well, yes, and there was also something more that made me believe your bog body was once at Loughshinny Fort."

They both leaned forward and waited for the next word, alert, and rigid with attention. This word was not going to escape the room without Maire and Sean hearing it first.

"Her tunic."

"What?" they both chimed in at the same time.

"Her tunic." Martin repeated the word as if it should all make sense to them now.

"What do you mean, her tunic?" Sean asked cynically. Now he was sure that Martin had lost all of his marbles.

"The Loughshinny hoard had the remnants of a cloak which was an exact match for the tunic your bog body was found in.

Maybe she was a Roman servant? Who knows, but the tunic and the cloak are exact matches." Martin looked from Maire to Sean to see what their reaction was. It was blank.

"Well. That's it, then," he said, slapping his hands on his thighs.

"No, no, no," Maire said, growing increasingly emphatic with each "no."

"I am afraid it is, Maire." Martin continued, "I knew that the coins were in her stomach because when I inquired about the CAT scan the specialist mentioned the three disks to me, and I asked to see the scan. I knew immediately from their size…, and the relief was fairly clear in one…, you could see the hills of Rome, so to speak, that they had to be the same coins."

"Impossible. You are lying again," Sean said, now shocked that he too was acting ballsy with Martin.

"I know this is frustrating," Martin said, while he rooted through files in his drawer and pulled out the black, white, and gray scan photograph. It had been enlarged, and the clearer coin had been zoomed in on. The second photo showed seven gray outlined hills on the circle of the clearest coin, clear as could be. There they were.

As Martin handed the photos over to Maire and Sean, he said, "That is how I knew the disks in her stomach were coins." "So she was at the Roman fort, and she swallowed three coins." Maire stared at the photos. "It doesn't help solve anything at all really, does it?"

"It only proves that she went there and then left," Martin nodded, "So looking through the Loughshinny hoard won't do you any good at all and again, just a reminder, you may not use this information in your presentation. She might have stolen the items and was being punished for it…, -who knows?"

He made a strange-looking face and shrugged his shoulders. "Hey! I have been waiting seventeen years for permission to examine the finds at Loughshinny! Don't expect any pity from me folks!"

"Well," Sean sighed, the mock relief raising his eyebrows a tad too high, and making his smile too big, "It's been great! Thanks for all the help." He stood up and left the office. Maire handed Martin back the photographs of the scans and shook her head in disbelief. "Red tape is just a pain in the arse!"

"I couldn't agree more," Martin answered, and stood up to shake her hand. "Sorry about yesterday. It was not my place to reveal the Loughshinny hoard to you. It would have meant my job, and I like my job."

"Understood," she said. "Will you be there for the rest of the presentation this afternoon?"

"I'd like to hear your findings and what the plans are for Mona," he said.

"Fair enough, we'll see you there." Maire knew that Mr. Martin was as frustrated as both she and Sean were. But he was right. A cloak that matched the one Mona was buried in did very little to clear up the motive for her murder. Maybe Mona was a thief; maybe she was the mistress of a Roman soldier or leader. The knowledge that a Roman hoard was being kept at the national museum really didn't answer why Mona had the same coins as the Roman find-in her stomach: another dead end, with no way to go but back.

Sean stood in the hallway stroking his chin and staring at his feet as if he had just seen them for the first time.

"I suppose he's right. All it proves is that she was there and then left." He didn't even try to hide his disappointment.

"Sure, you said the same thing yourself, Sean, less than an hour ago, when they agreed to let us take a break," Maire said, standing in front of him with her hands on her hips.

"Come on, then!" Sean piped up, "Let's get to work on that time machine and solve this mystery, you mad scientist, you!"
"We've solved nothing. We've just come up with more questions than answers, really."

They looked at each other, and without saying another word, they knew instinctively that this was the truth. They turned to walk back to the room where the presentation would continue. All they could do now was request how Mona would be displayed and that the photographs of the body being exhumed from the bog not be put on public display; they looked too grisly.

The body was too fresh looking, and it looked like a recent murder. There was no dignity in her death what so ever. Their argument would be to give her back what she lacked in her final moments, her dignity. When all the board members were seated, Maire began talking.
"We would like to continue where we left off-but we cannot."

Sean then spoke. "Due to the legalities of the Loughshinny find, we are unable to elaborate or conjecture further on what type of a life this woman lived shortly before she died."

He nodded at Maire, who instantly picked up where he left off, "Although we are certain that the clothing she wore was from the La Tène Celtic period, as another renowned Celtic specialist has assured us, due to the ornate gold trim, we also know that another garment identical to this design exists, but we are unable to say where."

"We also know," Sean added, "That the Roman coins found in her stomach are from a specific part of Ireland, but again we are bound by the law to leave this place unnamed in this presentation."

"So," Maire added, looking at Sean for approval, "We have presented all our findings. Mona was definitely an Iron Age woman who was murdered-, not sacrificed, but murdered-when she was approximately seven to eight months pregnant. Although the body had reddish hair when it was found, further investigation and scientific tests revealed that she had lightened her hair with lime and then styled it with a plant resin which we know grows in the north of Spain only. We know that she was eating a protein rich diet when she died, and that she probably died in early winter. This is also thought to be her time of death due to further scientific tests done on her hair and fingernails to determine protein levels in the body. We can speculate that her body was preserved in such good condition not only because of the sphagnum moss but also because she was buried in early winter and the ground froze quickly."

"Come up for air Maire," Sean said, shuffling uneasy beside her. Then he realized that Maire was fighting back tears. "I'll finish it," he said, and she nodded.

"Maire has suggested, and I fully agree, that due to the unbelievably good condition of this bog body it would be disrespectful and just plain fucking wrong, pardon my language, to display her as we do all the other bog bodies, as they were discovered." Now his voice had emotion in it.

"Display her lying down in her beautiful red tunic, the torc by her side, and only write how she was found and how she was buried. Don't even show the pictures of the body being exhumed."

Maire added a final statement. "Her death had no dignity to it. She was brutally tortured as a punishment, and buried in a spot that signified nowhere; not a kingdom, or land, or spiritual water, but nowhere. Display her with her dignity. She is an ancestor, not an artifact," Maire added, suddenly aware that there was too much emotion in her voice, that it sounded unprofessional. She began to distract herself by sorting the papers in front of her, not really sorting them at all, just shuffling them about.

"Thank you both for your excellent presentation and thorough research. We'll contact you both next week regarding our decision about her display. It seems to be of great importance to you both, so we will take it into great consideration."

After shaking everyone's hands, Maire and Sean made their way back to the lab. They both sat in silence for about ten minutes or more. Their minds were utterly drained of any thoughts except those of Mona. She had held them captive in their waking moments and their dreams for the last six months, and now their relationship with her was drawing to a close.

"What are you going to do tonight?" Sean asked.

"Sleep, after I have a chat with Rory," Maire answered.

Sean yawned, a lion sized yawn. "I need some serious sleep, too," was his reply.

By the end of January, the display was in place and the National Museum had tripled its number of visitors. Maire and Sean were both to view the display before the public was granted admission. It had been a long and exacting process to display Mona as they had requested. The Irish press had gotten wind of the bog body's nick-name, and for the weeks leading up to the revealing debut of Mona, the papers and television news declared,

"The most well-preserved bog body of all time to go on display at the National Museum in January." Even the RTE television journalist announced that she would be standing in line on the first day of the exhibit. Between the print news and television news, Mona's public debut was the talk of the country. Before any one set foot in the museum, Maire had a promise to fulfill. It was about six thirty on December 29 when Liam Hourigan answered the phone.

"Hello?" he said, with his gregarious Galway accent.

"Ah. Hello? This is Maire Moylan. May I speak with Liam Hourigan, please?"

"This is Liam Hourigan!" then he remembered why her name sounded familiar, "Oh, Jazus, the woman in the bog, is it?"

"It is indeed, Liam. The last time we spoke you indicated an interest in what we learned about the bog body you found almost six months ago. Would you like to be the first man, apart from the forensic archaeologists here at the museum, to see the woman that you found in Boteen's bog?"

"I would really love that. Name the time and the date and I will be there," Liam said.

"On January fourth at nine o'clock, Liam. Just call my office when you get to the museum, and I will come and get you. Okay?"

"Grand! Thanks a million for remembering to do this for me. I've been wondering since that day what her story would turn out to be. Now, what's the office number again?"
After telephone numbers and final good-byes had been given, Maire felt as if the story of this woman had come full circle. The man who found her would now see what this body looked like two thousand years ago. He too was going to come face to face with his own ancestor.

On January 4 at nine in the morning, Liam was standing beside the display case. His eyes were transfixed by red curly hair and the staring green eyes that peered past him from behind the glass of the display case. Mona was a stunning, serene beauty. She was lying down, as requested by Maire and Sean. Her superb red tunic, with its embroidered Celtic motif of gold trim recreated with exactness, glistened beneath the bright display case lighting. The torc, too, was reconstructed and worn as she would have worn it, not as a murder weapon. Her hands lay clasped in front of her at her waistline.

"This is how she would and should have been buried," Sean said, breaking the silence.

"Was she some sort of Celtic queen?" Liam asked absently as his eyes moved up and down the figure before him.
"No, we know that she was not a queen…, possibly higher up in the tribe than others, but her nails had slight striations which indicate that she labored, a little perhaps, so she was not a Celtic queen."
Maire's answer had a tone of disappointment in it that did not go unnoticed by Liam Hourigan.

"You don't sound too happy, Miss Moylan," he said, turning to look at her face.

"The day you found her was such an exciting day, Liam," Maire responded. "It has been a long haul for the last six months. Each forensic test we did revealed brutality after brutality. When you look at how she would have been, in her own time, and realize how brutally she was murdered, there is one thing that we lack, and it would shine more light on why she was brutally murdered. We lack a motive."

"She was murdered for no reason," Liam said nodding slowly.

"Science can only answer so many questions," Sean Sullivan added. "The rest is just hear say."

Chapter 11

Within moments her mouth was gagged. Her hands were tied behind her back. Outside she could hear children singing and women chattering as they walked across the wooden torch lit bridge toward the festival ground and blazing bonfire.

Liam Ruadh worked quickly to tie her into submission. In Élan's stomach, the volcano that longed to erupt could not do so. When she was bound and gagged, he swiveled her around to see his face.

He had returned for her.

"Now, here is my thinking, Élan. One promise to me has already been broken; the second shall be kept."

She shook her head and murmured beneath her mouth gag, an almost inaudible "No!"

"This bastard child in your stomach is not an Irish Celt, so it won't do. We don't need outsiders telling us what to do and marrying our women!" His eyes had the energy and movement of a mad man. The pupils were enlarged and alight with fire.

They waited until they heard no more feet trample on the wooden bridge; the last of the revelry makers had made their way to the feast.

Liam pushed her through the hut opening into the dark cold October air. So much noise and happy chatter was coming from the festival ground that no one paid any heed to the couple leaving the crannog and heading to the unhallowed ground.

The bonfire blaze tinted the night sky orange behind them. It faded to a soft glow as they left it in the far off distance. Beyond the bulrushes and heather was the unhallowed ground. Neither land nor water, neither fire nor air, the tribal boundary of two chiefdoms.

"Here is where a Celtic witch like you belongs. Nowhere," he hissed.

He stood in front of her and bent down to pick up a sally rod from the ground. Behind him was the soft sinking earth that had no end. Pools of water gathered in the shallows and showed the most treacherous spots. The sally rod was at once lashed across her ankles. She grimaced in pain and tears began to flow.

"Lift your tunic higher," he said as he rounded her to the front. She didn't lift her dress. "Let me assist you." The sally rod whipped her shins and lower legs several times, causing her to fall to her knees before him.

"Good," he said, "This is good." She shook her head, and her eyes pleaded with him.

"I have waited for this moment, Élan," he said.

The mouth gag was pulled down abruptly, and he kissed her sorely and harshly. As he pulled his face away, his fist rammed three Roman coins into her mouth. She cried but was muffled by handfuls of moist, damp soil.

"Payment, hag, payment for taking my Chieftain status away and not living up to your father's promise of being my wife! A traitor's payment for a traitor."

His hands were now around her neck, the torc giving way to the pressure and indenting itself into her skin.

"Not his wife, mine!"

By the time he released his grip she had been dead for some time. His breath was irregular and his hands felt as if they were paralyzed. When he pulled them away from her neck Élan fell toward him, her head resting at his waist. He grabbed her hair.

He dragged her body to the closest pool of water and staked it into the moist sinking ground by piercing her knees and ankles with the sally rod, and pinning her into the endless pit of damp soil, face first, pushing her down and waiting for the soft, watery ground to slowly devour her.

Slowly she sank into the earth. He stood to one side, on firm ground, watching as his months of planning had now come to fruition. The sally rod through the knees and ankles was to make sure she was anchored into the earth. Not to surface until he was well and truly safely back on the eastern shores of Ireland.

When the deed was done, he felt nothing. He stood momentarily and stared at the spot where he had hidden her. The soft land had swallowed her, and hidden her remains, and no one would find her now.

"Not of any tribe, not to land or water or air or fire do I commit the body of a traitor!"

He spit on the land, smiled, and turned away.

He began his journey back to the east coast and the tribe at Dun Laoghaire. Behind him the sky glowed orange and the sound of merriment filled the glowing sky; the festival of Samhain was truly under way.

Mona, the body in the bog

Acknowledgements

I want to thank my friend, and a very fine artist, Jeff Buckholz, for bringing the images in my head to life on paper.

The cover illustration, in particular, brings Mona's story into a vivid and harsh reality.

The map of Ireland on the interior pages shows the journey the Celts took from the crannog to Loughshinny.
The Roman coins and Celtic cloak pin illustrations, also by Jeff Buckholz, add another dimension to this story.

I thank those who read the book in its early and rather raw stages, for their suggestions and input; Judith and Pete for suggesting revisions, Robert for suggesting the use of the talented artist Jeff Buckholz, Arden for suggesting a map of Colm and Élan's journey across Ireland, in addition to a glossary for unknown words, Alice, Jay, Eileen and Gerry, many thanks for being generous with your time and reading the book. The biggest compliment you can give any writer is to read their book. Your encouragement and support are greatly appreciated.

Thank you.

Loretto

Glossary

Crannog- a partially or entirely artificial island, usually built in lakes, rivers and estuarine waters of Scotland and Ireland.

Imbolc- a Gaelic festival marking the beginning of spring.

Tánaiste -was originally the Irish word for the heir of the chief (taoiseach) or king.

Ogham stone- is an Early Medieval alphabet used primarily to write the Old Irish language, and the Brythonic languages.

Celts- or Kelts were an ethno-linguistic group of tribal societies in Iron Age and Medieval Europe who spoke Celtic languages and had a similar culture.

Samhain- is a Gaelic festival marking the end of the harvest season and the beginning of winter or the "darker half" of the year.

Definitions provided by Wikipedia

About the Author

Loretto Leary wrote *Mona, the Body in the Bog* because of her love for Celtic art and history, in addition to her interest in the preserved bog body finds now on display in the National Museum in Dublin.

She is an avid blogger, and her blog, Breise! Breise! Extra! Extra!, contains a plethora of her writings, and musings, and displays her love for the written word and journalism.

Loretto is a qualified K-6 and secondary teacher in language arts and is currently pursuing certification as a reading specialist due to her own passion for reading, hoping to instill that love of books in others. A native of Ireland, Loretto now lives in Connecticut with her husband and son.

To keep up to date with Loretto's publications visit her website at Lorettoleary.com

Loretto's next book *The Foundling,* and a short novella, *Outward Walls* are available at Amazon.com

Death and the Bereavement Group, Loretto's fourth book is due for release in August 2013.

To keep up to date with Loretto's work please visit her website Lorettoleary.com

Reviews of Mona, the body in the bog

"A Unique juxtaposition of parallel tales and times. Tana French, with a sense of humor."
C. Schack

" A really good read. The mystery begins when a body is found in a bog in Ireland during construction work. It follows the lives of Élan, a female tribal chieftain from 700 BC, and Maire, the modern-day forensic scientist who studies her, naming her "Mona". A little bit of archeology, science, history, superstition, and drama, all told with Loretto Leary's compassionate, intelligent voice. I instantly loved the characters in this story and found myself glued to the page in a way I haven't been for a long time. Appropriate for ages 13 and older; there is some sex, and some violence younger readers might find upsetting. Was Mona murdered, or was it an accidental death? Why did she die with three Roman coins in her mouth? Will Maire be able to solve the mystery? Read the book and find out."
J. Loukidis

"I loved it!! I love history. So I found the description of the day to day Celtic life really really interesting. I think you've given just the right amount of explanation, exactly where needed. Élan's fiery nature and strong character come across very clearly. I like the way that you shift back and forth between Élan's story vs. Mona's. It's interesting, because even though I knew how the book would end, I still wanted to keep reading till the very end. Keeps the reader guessing." D. Amin

15010152R00171

Printed in Great Britain
by Amazon.co.uk, Ltd.,
Marston Gate.